MW00877269

undercurrent
a novel by Jeff Schober

To Kim —
Thanks for reading this
with the Brocton Bookies.

Jeff S.
Oct 2008

Order this book online at www.trafford.com/07-1519
or email orders@trafford.com

Most Trafford titles are also available at major online book retailers.

© Copyright 2007 Jeffrey Schober.
All rights reserved. No part of this publication may be reproduced, stored in a retrieval
system, or transmitted, in any form or by any means, electronic, mechanical, photocopying,
recording, or otherwise, without the written prior permission of the author.

Note for Librarians: A cataloguing record for this book is available from Library
and Archives Canada at www.collectionscanada.ca/amicus/index-e.html

Printed in Victoria, BC, Canada.

ISBN: 978-1-4251-3812-7

*We at Trafford believe that it is the responsibility of us all, as both individuals
and corporations, to make choices that are environmentally and socially sound.
You, in turn, are supporting this responsible conduct each time you purchase a
Trafford book, or make use of our publishing services. To find out how you are
helping, please visit www.trafford.com/responsiblepublishing.html*

*Our mission is to efficiently provide the world's finest, most comprehensive
book publishing service, enabling every author to experience success.
To find out how to publish your book, your way, and have it available
worldwide, visit us online at www.trafford.com/10510*

www.trafford.com

North America & international
toll-free: 1 888 232 4444 (USA & Canada)
phone: 250 383 6864 ♦ fax: 250 383 6804
email: info@trafford.com

The United Kingdom & Europe
phone: +44 (0)1865 722 113 ♦ local rate: 0845 230 9601
facsimile: +44 (0)1865 722 868 ♦ email: info.uk@trafford.com

10 9 8 7 6 5 4 3 2 1

Grand Island

N

Fort Erie

Crescent Beach

The Hike

Lake Erie

CANADA
UNITED STATES

2 mi
2 km

Niagara River

Buffalo

NEW YORK

Hamburg

Hamburg Beach

undercurrent

a novel by Jeff Schober

1

In the heartbeat of time it took ice to collapse beneath Tony Davenport, his eyes jerked upward and witnessed clear sky. The blue was vibrant, and he was transported to days past, horizons he studied as an inquisitive child. Then the world was fresh, each dawn offering an opportunity to unearth some new-found treasure. The thought was his final moment of tranquility. Just before he fell, Tony heard a crackling sound, processing its meaning too late. There was no time to look down. He was swallowed by water. Arms and legs flailed, clothes absorbing wetness like a dry sponge, expanding across his limbs in a flash-flood of cold. His earlobes and nostrils submerged, smacking with sharpness. Skin on his face and neck burned with frigidity, a sensation so chilling he believed he was experiencing absolute zero.

While kicking ice chunks and fluttering toward the patch of light above, Tony thought, "I'm about to die."

He heard the girls' screaming before his head broke the surface. When it did, warm air offered little relief. Ice shards immediately froze around his nostrils. His throat was raw and dry. Shocked, disoriented, he forced himself to think clearly. His companions' hysteria added to confusion.

Victoria Maxwell shrieked with abandon. A few feet from where Tony submerged, her left leg had punctured ice, leaving her trapped like an animal in a snare. Her eyes were wide, and she flopped on her backside, right leg stretched flat. She remained paralyzed, afraid to move, unsure whether retreat would loosen ice around her.

Amy Black leaned toward Tony, her first impulse to offer an arm and pull him out. An ululating moan scraped the depths of her throat. But when she caught sight of a spider-web crack in a path where ice gave way to water, self-preservation took over. Widening her stance, she retreated, moving tentatively. She would have to solve this problem with logic, not thoughtless reaction.

"Tony, are you all right?" Amy called.

He didn't look at her but turned his head, unsure from where the sound emanated. "Goddamn, it's cold," he muttered. "Okay, now don't anybody panic." Amy watched his face bob. Slicked hair had darkened, and fear commandeered his brown eyes. She understood he did not know what he was saying.

"My God," Victoria screamed. "The ice is cracking." A sound like fracturing bones rumbled beneath her. She kicked her legs and began to scramble backwards in a crab walk.

"Victoria! Stay still!" Amy shouted, but Victoria was past the point of reason. As her left leg withdrew from its cavity, her right arm backed onto a patch of cloudy ice. Simultaneously a sharp clap of perforation pierced the air and her arm stabbed through into frigid water. She screamed as her hand and elbow vanished. Victoria's torso flopped horizontally on the thinned surface, surrendering control, moving involuntarily. She was in full panic mode, yanking her arm from the murky crater, flailing without rhythm or compunction. Jostling weight weakened the frozen field. As she struggled against invisible forces, thin ice shattered like tempered glass. She disappeared downward.

As Victoria fell, sound was swallowed with the body. There was a deafening moment of silence.

"No!" Amy raged with fear, heart contorting. "Victoria!"

Unlike Tony, Victoria did not bob to the surface. Seconds stretched. Five. Ten. Fifteen. Amy inched closer to the hollow, scanning open water for her friend. But veins of weakening ice kept her too distant to see into the depths.

"Victoria?" Tony murmured, swollen purple lips trembling. There was a lapping of water around his neck. He was confused, shivering. His voice sounded feeble. "Did she just go in?"

Amy turned toward Tony's face, blood drained so his features resembled a corpse, and watched him paw at the serrated edge, unable to maintain a grip without splintering off an ice chunk and opening the hole wider.

"Tony," she shouted, aware he was in shock. "Hold still. I'm going to find a firm patch and use my jacket to pull you out."

"Victoria," he called back, scanning from his low sight line. "Where is she? Did she go under?"

"I need you to stay calm. Let's get you out first," Amy replied, inching closer, removing her vest and extending it toward him.

"I've got to get her," Tony whispered, inhaling a deep lungful of air. He ducked under the surface, vanishing from sight.

"No!" Amy cried, afraid to move. "No!" She looked toward

the deserted Canadian shore, where dormant summer cottages loomed close enough that she could see the painted wooden slats of window shutters. Her eyes scanned the coast for some sign of movement, some hope of life. "Help!" she screamed. "Help! Help!"

There was no one within earshot. Her shrill cries were carried away, swallowed by the dull horizon.

2

By the numbers, Lake Erie is 210 miles long, fifty-seven miles across at its widest point, and has an elevation 571 feet above sea level. It is the shallowest of the Great Lakes, with a mean depth of sixty-two feet, plunging to 210 feet at its deepest spot. Its volume is 116 cubic miles; discharge at the eastern end of the basin is 202,269 cubic feet per second. Lake Erie retains its water for a mere two and a half years — the shortest span of any of its neighboring Great Lakes. By contrast, Lake Superior's retention time is 182 years.

Freshwater flows northeast through the elongated waterway, filtering through a narrowing mouth that funnels into the Niagara River. This necktie of water divides Western New York from southern Ontario. Here the two nations' landforms are positioned like puzzle pieces that do not fully interlock, water separating terra firma into geopolitical divisions.

The eastern edge of Ontario follows lazy meanderings of the Niagara River, its contour shaped like a novice art student's squiggly line, falling north to east, dimpling inward

in a shallow C so Grand Island can expand the river, like the
swollen belly of a snake after a fresh feed. Further south, just
across the narrowest river juncture — connected by the Peace
Bridge, a utilitarian 75-year-old span, where the Canadian
town of Fort Erie comes closest to kissing the city of Buffalo — the ridge of land takes an abrupt right turn. Heading west, the southern coast of Canada spans a descending
shallow line. Ten miles further, the Point Abino peninsula
extends its elbow into the lake, sheltering land to the east.

On the opposite side, a four-lane highway familiarly
known as Route 5 runs north-south along the American
shore, clinging to the water's edge as the landscape makes
a gradual southwest turn some eight miles below the city.
Beginning in Buffalo, driving south on Route 5, one would
cross an elevated skyway just outside of downtown, then see
a nature preserve (constructed atop an old landfill), cutout
concrete docks and abandoned grain elevators, a small boat
harbor, and brownfields that once housed a mighty steel
mill. Continuing south, into Hamburg, neighborhoods have
names like Athol Springs, Locksley Park and Mount Vernon.
Homes have been built on low-rising hills to face the great
lake, windows and porches positioned for waterfront viewing.

Here there is a narrow swath of sandy public beach.
During summer, it is open for swimming and sunbathing.
During the winter freeze, ice fishermen haul ATVs onto the
rugged ice and snow, spinning away from shore with augers
and deep angling gear.

Lake Erie is powerful, but its power is dormant, often
masked in beauty, and therefore can be misleading. To
gaze at the lake on a tranquil summer day is to see flatness,
sparkling, rich aqua hues. In winter, the frozen surface is a
hockey rink built to scale for the gods. Hardened ice belies

chugging currents below.

Nearby residents understand Lake Erie's petulance. They know an unwritten law: things absorbed by the lake may be disgorged from the lake. Expected items have washed on shore: dead fish, driftwood, trunks and branches of rotting trees. The lake also hurls unexpected things landward: bowling balls, finding their way atop the crest of waves to pierce the air like cannon fire, rotting cow carcasses, rusted automobile frames. Those who do not see these anomalies underestimate the lake's rawness.

In this international rectangle, much of the Canadian shore is sandy and smooth, a gentle incline between water and land. Canada is the lee side of westerly winds, and its beaches' names are familiar to residents: Crescent Beach, Crystal Beach, Sherkston Shores. Across the lake, the American shoreline is more often rugged and hard. What few beaches exist are smaller, sometimes man-made. South of Buffalo, in towns named Lake View, Derby and Angola, wind-whipped water batters rocky shores, etching steep cliffs into the landscape.

Here, when gusts increase, danger rises as well. Parts of Route 5 twist and contort, separated from the lake by a puny metal guardrail shielding a fifteen-foot drop. In winter, the highway may be closed when storms move in. Western New Yorkers are familiar with the term "lake effect," a phenomenon in which weather gains strength from the expanse of open water. Snow is dumped, soggy meaty flakes, at the rate of several inches per hour. At times, when fronts approach, visibility on the lake is reduced to mere feet, so water and sky are nothing more than a foggy opaque wall.

At such times, nature can be startling. Power lines are coated with ice, windblown smooth, into lava-like stalactite patterns. If air temperature drops suddenly amid strong winds, waves freeze quickly, each new splash of water melded to the hardening crest until the arc is taller than an amusement park slide. The beauty imposes its will upon curious onlookers, who are hypnotized and drawn to the ice field. Grandparents bundle up the little ones and venture onto the frozen landscape, urging wide-eyed children along, laughing while their tiny bodies explore nature's anomalies.

The lake is democratic, enchanting, oblivious to age or season. While its wonder is appreciated, its brute power can be overlooked. Too often, respect for the lake is forgotten, like whispered words on a windy day.

Lake Erie can be lethal.

3

The windows on his 1989 Dodge Dynasty had fogged over
while Tony Davenport waited in the parking lot. He was
uncomfortable in the car. By nature he was impatient, and
waiting in any form was wasted time. It didn't help that his
body did not easily conform to the limited space of a front
seat. He was 6'2", and seven years ago had been in peak condition, when he played linebacker in high school. But the day
he left home he fell into a college pitfall, eating fatty foods at
odd hours, abandoning his workout regimen. Now, at 25, he
generally felt fit, but had begun to grow a paunch. His back
was sometimes sore as well, and that made sitting for too
long an uncomfortable prospect.

A half hour earlier, he had aimed his car toward the
harbor, turned off the ignition — the heater and defrost
were on the fritz anyway — and watched ice fishermen haul
their bucketed gear onto the frozen plain. The sun was still
making its late morning ascent, and brightness reflected off
the snowy glaze. Within fifteen minutes, the car's windows
clouded with condensation, and Tony's view of the world

9

turned hazy. He saw everything as if peering through a thickening silk curtain, aware of shapes with fuzzy edges. Despite the winter jacket, inactivity of sitting left him cold. Exposed ear lobes turned numb, and his gloved fingers began to tingle.

This would be part of loving Victoria, he knew. Waiting. Amy and Tony joked that there was Eastern Standard Time and Victoria Standard Time. VST ran twenty to thirty minutes later. He could have arrived at 11:20 instead of the appointed time, budgeting for her lateness. But a hopeful part of him considered that after what transpired two nights before, she would be punctual, reluctant to make him wait, anxious to see him again. Those were emotions Tony felt, and he wanted her to as well.

The parking lot was blanketed with snow. A single lane had been plowed, exposing graveled blacktop. Floating wooden docks were removed for winter, stacked three deep. Nearby, a rusting crane shaped like a metal dinosaur pointed skyward.

Distant swooshes from cars passed on Route 5 behind the harbor. Otherwise, silence settled. A few scattered trees in the parking area were dwarfed by the expanse of frozen water.

How very odd, he thought. Ten months ago, if there was to have been romance, he was certain it should be with Amy. They were inching towards that, had even started to get physical, and then, in an instant, everything changed. Back then, he never would have anticipated falling for Amy's roommate.

Tony alternately watched the blurred harbor and glanced toward the roadway. Nearing 11:30, a faded maroon sedan turned into the parking lot. Tony's gloved hand smeared condensation from the windshield. His stomach fluttered, like after a first kiss, when he recognized Victoria's Oldsmobile. She parked to his right, turned off the ignition, and quickly transferred into his passenger's seat.

"Hi," she said, and before he could reply, she leaned across the center console and kissed him on the mouth. He felt a stirring in his thighs, remembering. Her lips tasted like strawberries, and he flattened his hand across the knit cap she wore, letting his left arm slide around her shoulders.

"What a night," she said. "I'm still a bit giddy."

"Me too," Tony grinned.

Who would believe the story? Neither Tony nor Victoria had told anyone yet — its suddenness left little time for anything else. But both of them delighted in the secrecy of their tryst, and Victoria reveled in its newness. There would be time later to sort out emotions and analyze details. For now the feelings were unpredictable, like an amusement park ride that contorted gravity. At any moment, something might shift unexpectedly.

Tony thought of his best friend, Mark, who would be the first person he told. It would be an awkward confession, difficult to explain. Tony had known Victoria for three years, as a platonic friend, and suddenly thunder crashes, skies open, and feelings gush like a monsoon? How could he tame that into words? Could he convince Mark of the stark emotions he felt for Victoria? Mark would devour him with questions, and analysis was not something Tony was ready for.

Looking at Victoria sitting in his passenger's seat, Tony wondered why it had taken so long to reach this point. How could attraction be so strong and deliberate, when he had barely noticed her the first time they met? It had been at Amy's apartment, he remembered that, and Amy had walked him through the kitchen, stopping near the sink to introduce her roommate. Victoria's hands were submerged in sudsy water, so he did not offer to shake. Tony nodded cursorily, mumbled a greeting, and followed Amy away. He had not given her another thought that day.

Now, on a sunny, crisp Saturday, three years later, Tony and Victoria were basking in the dawn of spending a night together.

"Good directions. I've never been here," she said, nodding toward the breakwall.

He leaned across the gear shift, kissing her again. "The name isn't that creative: Small Boat Harbor. It's a bit obvious. But you're going to love this."

She met his lips and held them, feeling stubble brush her chin before letting go and speaking. "I don't know. I'm not much of a daredevil."

"Neither am I. But this isn't an adrenaline rush, like jumping from an airplane. I can't even describe it. It's... I guess... it's a slow, quiet euphoria of freedom. Just you and God out here. You're walking on His water. Granted, it's frozen, but still a taboo. I can't really do it justice with words."

"You're sure this is safe?" Victoria asked.

"Absolutely." He turned left and aimed a finger southward. "I grew up just down the road. When I was in high school, kids used to take six-packs out on the ice all the time. You'd go far enough from shore that no one could see what you were doing. As long as it was cold, there was never any problem. Heck, Larry Erikson even drove his rusty pickup truck out there."

"He survived?"

"Oh yeah. He was disappointed the truck didn't fall in. It was such a heap of junk. Apparently the insurance was worth more than the actual truck. Every morning he'd come into first period and say, dammit, the ice held. You guys want to help me fill the bed with rocks and I'll take it back out after school?"

Victoria grinned at Tony's exaggerated hillbilly accent. Her eyes slid skeptically to the harbor before her. "Still…"

Tony smiled convincingly. "Do you see those fishermen?" He nodded toward the dozen silhouetted dots, faceless men sitting on buckets, some sheltered behind plastic lean-tos, solitary in their pursuit. From the distance, their poles were gossamer thin, too fine to be seen unless sunlight glistened off the moving tips. "They're out there every day, perched like it's the most natural thing in the world. They know when the ice isn't safe anymore. We'll be fine, I promise. If there was any doubt, I wouldn't even consider it."

Victoria adjusted her knit cap downward, covering her forehead. "I'll trust you. But I'm still going to be scared."

"Don't be. I'm here."

She smiled, getting out of the car. His glove encircled her puffy mitten as they walked the shallow descent onto ice.

Victoria Maxwell had the confident stride of an athlete. Her body was lean, appearing taller than her 5'6" frame. Beneath the knit toque, hair was the neutral color of autumn bark, lighter near the tips, and she parted it in the middle, folding long tendrils into the crook of her ears.

Victoria's beauty was subtle. Tony believed it would blossom with changing seasons. When they first met, Victoria seemed ordinary in his eyes. He found nothing noteworthy about her face, and did not consider her as anything more than Amy's roommate, shy and polite. At a Christmas party, Tony had a chance to talk with Victoria for longer than the curt hellos and goodbyes they had exchanged in the past. It was then, in an otherwise forgettable conversation about the winter Olympics, he noticed Victoria's chestnut eyes. He felt they absorbed things with inquisitiveness, quickly digesting information and transforming into knowing wisdom. Pointed nostrils contrasted with a shallow bridge of nose and smooth skin. Her beauty, Tony thought, was like 3-D art: at first, you did not notice it, but when you searched the right place, for the proper amount of time, it gradually sharpened into focus, plain to see.

They followed a tamped path through snow. Laying their boots on existing footprints, Victoria hesitated when they reached the blurred edge of land and ice.

"Ready?" Tony asked, face bright with enthusiasm.

"Rrrr," Victoria growled, both nervous and excited. "I'm scared, but let's do it."

Tony released Victoria's hand, striding boldly onto the frozen water, taking several confident steps before pivoting. He extended his arm, inviting Victoria.

"Come on," he said.

She stepped tentatively where he had just been and laid her mitten in his glove. He was heavier than her, she knew, and if ice supported him, there was really no danger. Still, reluctance, a nagging pang of conscience, echoed in her brain: I should not be here. Those who walk on a frozen lake are tempting fate, defying nature's law.

The couple strolled the harbor's perimeter without disturbing fishermen. After making a half loop, tracing the rock-littered arm of the breakwall, they cut back in a crooked line, leaving space between themselves and the anglers.

Within minutes, Victoria's fears evaporated. She grew giddy again, enamored with the flat crunching sound of rubber soles against the brittle. Its novelty and newness emboldened her. Clean air drew into her lungs. The purity increased her heartbeat. Cheekbones tingled in winter's chill. Senses heightened with reverence and awe. This was a new, invigorating perspective. Here, from this strange vantage, anything was possible.

"This is amazing," she said softly.

Tony enjoyed it too, but his thoughts had turned to Amy. If not for Thursday night, their friend would have been invited today. Tony worried about Amy's fragility. How would she respond to the news he slept with her roommate?

"We're going to have to tell Amy, you know," he said dully. "She deserves to hear it from us."

Victoria halted, sensing the shift in mood. She turned from shore and gazed past the breakwall's edge toward Lake Erie. "Yeah."

"How do you think she'll react?"

Victoria exhaled, pushing away uncomfortable breaths. Between romance and nature's baptism, somber words tasted reluctant. "Who knows? I guess worst case scenario is that it could be the end of our friendship."

4

At twenty-eight years old, Amy Black had aged during the past twelve months — aged enough that she appeared a decade older, if not more. Her shoulders, once square, erect and proud, had hunched forward, rounding toward her chest, and pouches of flesh sagged beneath cloudy eyes. Her body displayed fewer curves now, and her face wore a stolid mask. She was always big-boned, but until recently, had not projected an aura of heaviness. Her 5'9" frame helped offset the weight. During the past year, that largeness had morphed into something unformed. She began to wear roomier clothes, shaped like sacks of rice — sweaters that were wide and sagged off her neck, with enough girth around the stomach to disguise any additional flab.

Most of her friends could pinpoint an exact moment the transition began, but were surprised that its effects permeated so many facets of her life. The shock began innocently, like spilled wine. Nearly a year later, pores had yet to fully flush.

On March 24, 1993, a Wednesday, Amy had been attending a seminar on Edgar Allan Poe at the University at Buffalo. The department secretary had knocked on the door, interrupting the professor's lecture, and handed a small pink slip to the frail scholar at the head of the table. The man frowned, read the paper over the edge of his glasses, and said in a timid voice, "Amy Black, you need to call your mother. She has an emergency message for you."

Amy's heart thumped with foreboding as she slid away from the desk. Her brow furrowed considering possibilities. The secretary held the door ajar with an expression of concern, and invited Amy to follow through the narrow hallway toward the office phone.

Her mom answered, but before Adele Black spoke, Amy heard the tears. The strain stiffened her shoulders and arms.

"Amy, my God. There's been an accident with your dad."

"An accident? What kind of accident?"

A primitive sob came through the phone, peppered by short breaths.

"Mom? What's going on?"

Mini convulsions, gasps like gunfire. "Your father. Oh God, Amy."

"Are you alone? Is anyone with you?"

"I found him in the garage," she said shakily. "I called 911, then your apartment. Victoria said you were in class. She's on her way to pick you up."

Amy stood mutely by the secretary's desk, trying to process the news. Cradling the phone, she studied the spiraling black cord and the way it contrasted against eggshell colored walls. There were no pictures or hangings to interrupt the monotony. The room was blocky and cold. This stupid campus was so damn bland, absent of color or vibrancy, and Amy found herself suddenly mad at the lack of feeling that surrounded her, engulfed in banality.

Her mother wailed into the phone. Nearby, the secretary had turned her back to Amy, sorting files from an adjacent cabinet. The older woman was eavesdropping with heightened senses, but did not wish to appear intrusive. She was ready, however, for a sudden breakdown from Amy; prepared to offer a sympathetic shoulder. Amy knew it, and stubbornly did not want to provide such satisfaction.

Details sifted clear over the next several hours: her father had been in the garage working underneath his car when the jack slipped, pinning him. No one had been nearby. Adele arrived home with groceries to discover the scene.

With flashbulb clarity, Amy remembered events in the week that followed: the extended family returning from points far away, gathering in their wallpapered kitchen and speaking in hushed tones about Richard Black's virtues. She went to a department store with her mom to shop for the suit in which her father was to be buried. The absurdity, the sense of surreal, was not lost on Amy: she could not recall the man ever wearing a suit. He had a tattered hound's tooth jacket he donned for weddings, but Amy's mother never liked it, told her husband often enough that it was "dumpy and outdated." The women chose a black pinstriped outfit and formal shoes whose color matched. With the suddenness of death and chaotic burial plans, Amy knew her mother felt control slipping away — but the one thing she could ensure was that the man she loved was properly attired as he headed into the afterlife.

Once funeral proceedings ended and the family scattered again, Amy Black's life became a washed-out haze. She remembered little of the next several months.

Before her father's death, there were a few guys who interested her. Amy had been on three dates with a wiry doctoral candidate named Roger. He was quiet and soft-spoken, but they had not yet spent enough time together for Amy to decide whether she could commit to him. Somewhere, in those ensuing months, they stopped seeing each other. Amy could not remember when or if an actual conversation around that ending ever occurred. She simply realized one day that he was no longer part of her life. Had he even attended the wake? She could not recall.

There were also feelings toward Tony, which complicated the situation with Roger. Amy and Tony were friends, yes, but he was cute and charming, and briefly, for the first time since they had known each other, both were unattached. One winter night, more on impulse than anything, she kissed him. She intended to force the question: could their friendship develop into something more?

Amy's romantic overtures slammed like blocks of cinder when her father died. After that, nothing mattered like it did before.

When she was aware of frost blanketing the ground, Amy realized the days had morphed into October. She had no recollection of spring, or summer holidays like July 4th, Labor Day. Without her dad, a long-delayed shock ate away at chunks of time. Life drifted, and she was largely oblivious to it.

* * *

One Friday night in November, seated on opposite ends of the couch in Tony Davenport's apartment while a Bruce Willis movie played on TV, Amy Black whispered, "I wonder what his last moments were like. When the jack slipped and the Corvette collapsed onto his chest, did he know he was about to die?" Her blue eyes widened, filming with moisture as tears gathered in their edges.

Tony turned from the blaring TV. He studied Amy's anxious face with confusion. They had not been speaking about Amy's dad — in fact, Tony focused on TV skyscrapers and terrorists so intently that for a time he forgot Amy was even there. But she had watched the small screen blankly, without processing its images.

"I thought the doctors said he died instantly," Tony offered.

"Maybe they were just saying that to ease our grief."

"He didn't know anything hit him. He never suffered. That's what you were told, right?"

Tears leaked from the corners of her eyes. "Yeah. But how can a doctor know that for sure? Maybe it took thirty seconds for his heart to stop beating. Do you know how long thirty seconds really is? He could have been lying there pinned that whole time, paralyzed, unable to call for help, knowing there was nothing he could do but wait for death."

Tony recognized Amy's pain, sympathizing in silence. He leaned across the sofa cushion, resting his hand firmly on her knee. It remained while she lowered her forehead, pressing it to his arm and sobbing.

* * *

Amy Black's friendship with Tony Davenport was one of the things that kept her connected to the world after her dad's passing. In the three years they had known each other, their relationship had been an arc of ascending trust: each month, they became closer, more familiar.

They met during a spring seminar at the University at Buffalo. The pair shared a dislike for the professor, and made snide comments about him before and after class. Tony invited Amy to a barbeque when the weather warmed; she reciprocated by asking him to a Memorial Day picnic. There was never overt romance between them. During the seminar, Tony had a girlfriend, and by the time that relationship ended, Amy and he had firmly established themselves as buddies, not potential mates.

He enjoyed her casualness. Rarely was conversation forced — Amy simply said whatever was on her mind, without forethought or motive. She would discover a strand of hair lying on the sofa, pick it up and examine it under light. Her eyes would narrow, studying its texture and color. After pausing for a moment, she would declare, "It's one of yours," and casually toss it on the floor. This never failed to elicit a chuckle. Tony always wondered how she might act if she discovered the hair was her own — preserve it in a baggie for DNA cloning?

She was drawn to him because of his steady temper. Too many of her female friends were moody, their personality changing with each new weather pattern. He was never flustered or hurried, but even, reliable. He had never pulled an all-nighter, he said, because he would not allow himself to fall that far behind in his studies. Dependability was a lost trait in the ever-bustling world, Amy knew. Tony was a welcome exception.

* * *

With the calendar's turn into 1994, Amy Black was tired of wallowing in sorrow. Since the previous spring, she had felt morose, a thick wool curtain descending across her world. Depression would need to evaporate before she could function with any sort of normalcy. Her father had died in March, nearly a year ago; plenty of time for the grieving process to run its course, she thought. The new year, full of resolutions and hope and fresh beginnings, was a natural segue to focus on the future, not the past. Her dad would have wanted her to continue looking ahead. Still, it was easy to decide depression should be over, far harder to implement the change. If sadness could be flipped off like a light switch, the world would be a simple place. Amy had a plan: she intended to make a determined effort each day to appreciate the positive aspects of life. She needed to rediscover the goodness that touched her regularly, and savor its presence.

Such events became illuminated when she taught. In spite of her inner turmoil, at work she was able to maintain composure, donning a mask of professionalism. Departments were in upheaval, administrators were fleeing to better jobs in neighboring districts, and there was pressure from the superintendent and board of education to improve student test scores. At least once a month, a memo was circulated outlining a new plan of action. Veteran teachers griped and complained, filing grievances with the union. But Amy was able to compartmentalize those outside pressures, push them aside, and focus on her students. Something as simple as a popular kid being nice to a geek could brighten Amy's day. Little things like that, she reasoned, illustrated how people can be good. Her task was to seek out and appreciate those events, however minor.

But away from school she grew overwhelmed. The world was rushing past. Often she felt her mind and body were slipping off the edge of a spinning carnival ride. Immersed in law school, responding to its academic challenges, her room-mate Victoria was brimming with energy. In contrast, Amy's free time was spent sleeping long hours and watching TV. She could not match Victoria's daily enthusiasm and tried to avoid her. Amy wanted to be left alone.

The Black family owned a summer cottage in Canada, just across the Peace Bridge, in the Crescent Beach neighbor-hood of Fort Erie. Although bustling in summer, the lakeside community was nearly deserted during colder months. A fifteen minute ride from her apartment, Amy began spend-ing weekends there in the fall; by January, she had added two or three weeknights as well.

Isolation was soothing. It allowed her time to reflect, with-out the peering eyes or interruption of a roommate. There was no one asking how she felt that day, no implied judg-ment that she stayed in bed too long or didn't eat a healthy dinner. Often, she reveled in the early darkness. After day-light vanished at 5 p.m., lights remained off, and she trudged through the shadowy cottage carrying a lone candle.

In those weeks of retreat, Amy came to recognize that one of the most steady, meaningful parts of her life was the friendship shared with Tony Davenport. There were mo-ments when she had felt closer to him than anyone else. He had supported her in the past year, serving as a platform for her failing psyche, calling daily, making sure she was never alone for too long. She was always included in his weekend plans, and he made a point to visit if they had gone longer than a week apart. He was, by definition, a true friend.

Since her self-imposed withdrawal, she began to consider a question she had pondered only briefly a year earlier: could it be that Tony entered her life for a different reason than simply friendship? Amy vacillated about her growing feelings for him. He was attractive, she argued with herself, in an "everyman" sort of way. Tony had shown her pictures from high school, when he was trim and fit, eyes sparkling brightly with fresh-faced, naïve anticipation of the future. Seven years later, he had grown chubby, scruffy with his grunge look, but seemed more relaxed than those earlier photos suggested.

Her father's death was such a turning point that Amy's memories of kissing Tony seemed distant, like they occurred on the lee side of another life, beyond the ridge of sight. With the Corvette's collapse, a dividing line was marked. Everything before then seemed foggy, comical, almost childish.

It was Saturday night, she remembered that. She and Tony went to a movie, an underwater leviathan drama so unbearable that within minutes they were whispering sarcastic jabs and stifling laughter, ignoring the glares around them. It was a waste of six bucks, they agreed, and trekked back to Amy's apartment. Victoria was in Toledo for the weekend. Amy poured herself a glass of white wine, uncapped a beer for Tony. He sat down at the living room piano and touched its keys. He had not played for several months, yet notes came easily to him, filling the room with warmth. Amy and Tony sang a few torch songs, old standards like the kind covered by Sinatra and Tony Bennett, trying to harmonize with one another's voices.

She was not drunk, but wine had pushed her toward the crest of euphoria. After playing piano, they sat at opposite ends of the couch, facing each other, legs intertwined across the center cushion. And in a moment of... what? — desire? weakness? over-stepping boundaries? — she swung her legs to the floor, pushed herself into his space, and locked lips. He seemed startled, surprised, even tentative. After ten seconds of initial shock, he fumbled, setting his beer bottle on the floor and raising a hand to her hair, brushing it away from their melded cheeks.

The embrace did not last long. Amy broke contact, leaned back, and through half-closed lids, saw his eyes were shut. He grinned dumbly, like a boy who has just learned a secret. Without speaking she took her empty glass to the kitchen.

It was a burst of sentimentality — brief as the time it takes for fireworks to fade from the sky — but that had been their only foray into love.

Unsure how to make the transition toward further romance — even more unsure if it was the proper thing to do — Amy hesitated. This relationship is complex, she thought. For us to move from friends to lovers, I need to examine the nuances.

Maybe. For now, just maybe.

5

No matter how he visualized and practiced, Tony Davenport's mind could not oil the conversation to remove discomfort:

Her stare was unnerving. Cold, judgmental, dripping with disdain. Shoulders tense, body rigid, eyes firing silent fury.

"You and Victoria," Amy repeated. Slowly, like someone tasting a foreign food for the first time, she asked, "Where?"

"Where?" Tony echoed, confused. "Where did this happen?"

"Oh. You mean, the first time?"

Her eyes, crestfallen. "How many times have there been?"

He stumbled, recognizing he misspoke. Today he could say nothing right. Tony had not wanted this revelation to be shattering. He had hoped to avoid this scene. Thought maybe, best-case scenario was that Amy would chuckle, express surprise, then mutter something about having suspected all along. Tony had been at their apartment often, so he and Victoria had spent time together, she knew that. In Amy's absence, well… they were both grown-ups. Both caring, generous people with common interests and a common friend and it was only natural they should develop romantic feelings. Amy would hug him in congratulations, and their lone awkward overture toward emotion would be released into a shallow stream, float away, unacknowledged and forgotten.

That was the script he would have written.

The other extreme tilted toward stereotype, and that was not Amy: a woman scorned. Plates and cutlery exploding against the wall in a cannonfire of kitchen supplies. Screams, wails of anger, accusatory tones punctuated by staccato finger pointing. How could you do this to me? How could you be so goddamn callous?

Instead, Amy's reaction flumed down the middle… a tense winter freeze.

"Here?" she wondered. "Did you and Victoria make love here? In my apartment?"

Tony said nothing, averting his gaze toward the couch's skirt.

"So let me get this straight," her voice was hardened concrete. "You kiss me on this very couch, my dad dies four days later, and then, while I'm mourning, while I'm a husk of a person, you sleep with my roommate?"

"Hey," Tony's hands went into a defensive posture. "Let's be honest: you kissed me. I did not make the first move."

"You kissed back."

"I didn't walk away, no. But if we're going to talk about this, let's at least be straight. I didn't know what that kiss was all about, and I'm not sure you did either. A year later, I still have no idea."

They glared at each other in silence, Tony searching for understanding, Amy overwhelmed.

"Maybe you had too much wine and I had one beer too

many," Tony confessed. "We kissed. But that moment — whatever it was either of us was thinking — was not what this relationship is about. What we have is based on friendship, not romance. Deep in our hearts, we both know that. And then, after you kissed me, we never spoke about it."

"My dad died," Amy spat. "I wasn't exactly in a state of mind where I could just—"

"I know. I get that. It's just that… well, it's not like we were even dating. We're friends. Friends who kissed. It was a kiss, that's it. It didn't… it didn't mean…"

"It didn't mean anything?" she asked.

"No, not that. I don't mean it like that. We were caught in a moment. But there was no promise, no understanding it would lead to more. And that's okay. You obviously had other things to worry about. But let's be real. I haven't been hanging around on the promise that you'll kiss me again. There was no implication to that kiss, and we both know it."

Conversation always ended with him reaching resolution — which he had arrived at last summer, long before sleeping with Victoria — that his kiss with Amy was an aberration. It was a momentary flash fueled by late-night intoxication and too much time spent together among single friends. Yet what would be Amy's resolution? As often as he turned the voices over in his head, he could never predict her final words; never felt comfortable assessing her mood.

He wanted more options.

* * *

Tony Davenport liked options. The problem was that sometimes he was inundated with too many. Even as a boy, he held a variety of disconnected interests, finding it hard to choose a favorite. Over the years, he came to realize this made for good conversation. He could meet someone at a barbeque and speak with reasonable intelligence about diverse topics. He was also outstanding at trivia games. Yet being a "jack of all trades, master of none" made for some difficulty in choosing a career.

He was by nature a curious person, intrigued with everything. In high school, kids would talk about their favorite subjects or favorite teachers, while vilifying others. Tony felt uncomfortable when lunch table conversations turned in this direction — he liked all his classes. Physics was equally as interesting as English. His teachers, too, had unique personalities, each different from one another. Some were old, some silly and goofy, some aloof and all business, but each was there to serve a purpose. As far back as elementary school, he considered a career in teaching. Tony recognized a teacher's role in shaping young people, and that appealed to him.

Such acceptance drove his friends crazy. Mark Jablonski would say, "How can you like all your classes? Wood shop rocks and social studies sucks! C'mon... that's a no-brainer, Tony."

Tony was never consumed by sports, but because of his size, was asked by the coach to play high school football. He enjoyed the camaraderie, took pleasure from competition, was impressed with the way training sculpted his body. He knew he lacked the talent or drive to be a professional athlete, but for a time thought maybe he could join the ranks of coaching.

He was not a stereotypical steroid-crazed jock. During summers he earned money by renovating houses with an uncle who lived on Buffalo's West Side. He learned about construction and came to appreciate the history of older homes. Tony enjoyed the challenge of updating — taking something from the past and modernizing it for another generation's use. He considered becoming a contractor.

Since age 8, he had taken piano and guitar lessons so that by high school he was a passable musician. The drama director needed someone who could pluck the notes to "Greensleeves" onstage, so Tony won a bit part. Should he focus on acting or become a professional musician? He had a sliver of talent that was showcased in neighborhood jam bands. If he worked hard and concentrated, musical skills would improve. For a time he bounced from band to band, playing as many Steve Miller covers as he could.

On Sunday mornings, Tony taught religious instruction — jokingly referring to it as "religious destruction" — to grade school kids. Briefly he wondered about joining the clergy, but ruled it out after recognizing that he liked girls too much to take the vow of celibacy required by the Catholic Church.

In college, there had been a class trip to Paris during spring break. This led to consideration of a career as a translator or linguist. A steady diet of Balzac novels in the original French fanned the flames, even if the language was sometimes confusing. (He preferred reading them in French because the few English translations he found lacked the same punch.) But his interest in France waned when he returned to Western New York and was unable to speak conversational French with anyone outside of class. To foster and fan the flames of a Francophile, he needed immersion.

By the beginning of his third year of college, Tony had yet to declare a major. At the University at Buffalo, he kept signing up for courses that seemed interesting without worrying about specific requirements. He was drawn, compass-like, to humanities classes. By the middle of his fourth year, he had accumulated enough credits for an English degree. The concept of teaching had always appealed to him. He did not want to be a perpetual student, so teaching English seemed the path of least resistance. In truth, he became a teacher only because he couldn't commit to anything else.

Standing before a grade seven classroom as a student teacher, all the other options peeled away. Tony stopped second-guessing himself, confident no other career beckoned from a distance. He loved teaching, loved the interaction with students, and knew his responsibility was to shape young lives.

His feelings toward Victoria were similar — there was a single-mindedness, a laser light projected from his heart. He had dated girls before, felt the pangs of adolescence. By his 20s, his interest turned lassiez-faire. Women provided bursts of pleasure, yet he recognized that immaturity — either his or the girl's — would muddle the future. For as much as he was attracted to women, no one ever put a stranglehold on his soul.

And suddenly, Victoria.

In a short time, everything came together. Tony felt like he was approaching some sort of peace, both professionally and personally. Perhaps, he reflected, that was the wrong phrase to use — there had ever been inner turmoil. He was always comfortable with the world, but could never really locate his unique place in it. In the past year, clutter receded. Billowing snow and ice were plowed aside and a clear, chaste path revealed itself: he would teach kids and love Victoria Maxwell.

But he needed to deal with Amy.

6

Tony Davenport had a comfort with women that eluded
Mark Jablonski, his best friend. Mark knew many girls, but
the relationships were distant, polite — certainly nothing
like the closeness Tony shared with Amy Black and Victoria
Maxwell. Mark knew that no woman would call him at 3
a.m. for help replacing a flat tire. Amy had asked exactly that
from Tony on a humid overnight the previous August, and
when Tony told him the story a few days later, Mark realized
that no one — male or female — would consider dialing his
number in that situation. It was telling, Mark recognized;
his relationships did not run deep enough to be considered a
"go-to" guy when emergencies arose.

Mark did not resent his friend, but sometimes a hint of
jealousy tingled in his stomach. Tony was good-looking,
Mark had to admit, albeit a bit chunky and disheveled. But
Mark was no gargoyle himself — he was taller, fair haired,
and slender. At twenty-five, he had maintained his high
school weight, something Tony had not been able to do.
Mark's neck and cheeks were still narrow, without the onset

of jowls to emphasize aging. Mark looked like a young man should, although perhaps closer to twenty than twenty-five, he thought. But women today were not drawn to pale, fresh faced kids — they wanted a guy who was swarthy or exotic.

Mark found himself reserved in company of the fairer sex, and he wasn't sure why. Lack of confidence? he wondered in moments of self-reflection. Probably not. He was as secure as the next guy. Maybe he was simply trying too hard. He yearned for women to desire him, to be intrigued by his breezy presence. He secretly longed for a girl to notice him from across a beachfront restaurant and think, who is that guy? He is someone I want to know. And Mark would display casual disinterest, only conversing with her after she trekked across the patio and sought him out. That fantasy had not blossomed yet, but it would be the ultimate compliment to Mark should it occur.

Most of Mark's daydreams involved women, summer, or a combination of the two. Now, on a chilly February evening, he was fixating on warmer days while he and Tony watched a hockey game, sharing pizza and beer.

"Why do I live in Buffalo?" Mark asked rhetorically. "It's cold here nine months of the year. I should move to Tampa. I'm not kidding. I need heat. I got to get out of this city."

"I thought you wanted to start a band this summer," Tony said. "You've been talking about it since September. I blocked out July and August to play guitar with you, but if you're not serious, tell me now. I'll rearrange my schedule to take sailing lessons or something."

"Sailing? Since when do you want to start sailing?"

Tony hesitated. "Victoria said she might want to."

"Okay, that's Victoria," Mark echoed. "Why do you want to do it?"

Quickly, without pomp or fanfare, Tony broke the news to his friend that he had slept with Victoria Maxwell five days earlier. Mark's face transformed to a bewildered grin. He was stunned, dumbfounded, flabbergast.

"You slept with Victoria?" Mark repeated, incredulously. "How did you pull that off?"

Tony shrugged. "It wasn't like I had some advance plan. We were hanging out and it sort of just happened."

"It sort of just happened? Things like that don't just happen."

"It did."

"Come on, give me more than that!"

"Well, we had been spending time together for the past few weeks, without Amy. I felt a little chemistry, but I didn't say anything, just in case I was wrong."

Mark interrupted Tony, his voice building with excitement. "You've known her how long? Three years? And you're just now sleeping with her? This is unbelievable! You've completely overridden the statute of limitations!"

Mark was notorious among their friends for barroom lectures about dating minutia, where he could elaborate crackpot theories about modern women. What it lacked in common sense or practicality, it made up for in humor. One of his favorites was the "statute of limitations."

"If you don't make a move on the girl within the first month you know her, all bets are off," he had said. "Dating is like a military strike: you've got to get in quick and let her know you're there. Put her on the defensive right away. Make your presence felt. The key word is impact. Appeasement didn't work with Hitler, and it's sure not going to work with women sixty years later. After a month of doing nothing, you're off a girl's radar screen."

Now, sitting in Mark's living room, beer cans open, two wedges of pizza hardening in the cardboard box, Mark's so-called wisdom had been disproved again.

"You realize that whole statute of limitations theory went out the window when Amy kissed me last year," Tony said.

"I didn't throw it out the window," Mark argued. "That was a blip on the screen. A fluke. In fact, I argue that the theory held up because nothing ever really happened between you two. Victoria, now that took some planning."

"I didn't plan it, really," Tony protested.

"You didn't plan it? The first time you sleep with this beautiful girl that you've known forever, and you say you didn't plan it? You're unbelievable!"

Mark's jaw closed long enough to focus on his TV, where a goal had just been scored in the hockey game. The thin man stood, playfully socked Tony on the shoulder with congratu-lations — was it because the Sabres scored or because I con-nected with Victoria? Tony wondered — then picked up the Coors can and shook to see if it was empty.

"Need another?" he asked, walking toward the kitchen.

"I don't know," Tony replied halfheartedly.

"Sure you do. We're going to sit here, turn the volume down nice and low and nurse our beers while you give me details about how you hooked up with Victoria Maxwell. Shit, man, I didn't even know you had a thing for her."

Tony grinned sheepishly, focusing on the TV. "You always said she was beautiful."

"Hell yeah, she's beautiful. She's like a black and white Audrey Hepburn. Old style class. I've had a thing for her since you introduced me at your 4th of July party. She hated that I kept calling her Vicky Max, remember? That's when I knew I didn't have a shot. What was that, like two years ago?"

"I guess."

"You guess. Look at you, sitting there all smug." Mark placed a chilled can in his friend's palm and returned to the lounge chair, leaning back and elevating his feet. "When did you become this casual? Is this what happens when you find a new crush?"

"I don't know, Jabber. This one feels different."

"Different? What do you mean?"

"I don't know. With Victoria, it feels right. Real, you know, like I'm not kidding around this time."

Mark studied his friend, then focused on the TV. He objected to Tony's serious turn, but didn't say anything for a long moment.

"You're in the early days of puppy love," Mark offered. "Of course it's going to feel right. If there wasn't chemistry, you never would gotten to this point. Every girl seems perfect in the first few weeks. You last a month or more, then you start seeing little flaws. At a restaurant, she'll use the fork tine to chisel food from her teeth, right in front of the matre d', and you'll have an internal debate about why you were ever attracted to her. That's about the time that she'll start trying to change you, too." In falsetto, he crooned, "Tony, tuck your shirt in. Do you have to wear flannel again? Make sure your shoes are tied."

Tony grinned to himself. Here we go again: Mark's zany dating theories. The guy has just about zero experience, yet lectures like he's Dr. Ruth. Tony recalled the time his friend approached a girl in a bar and said, "Hi, my name is Milk. I could do your body good."

"This is different," Tony protested.

Mark scoffed. "Yeah, everybody thinks their romance is

different."

"Ours is. Victoria and I already know each other. Because of Amy, we've been friends for three years. There aren't any big secrets or surprises between us. I know some of her quirks already. Here's one: she's late all the time. I'm sure I'll discover more, but right now, I accept that about her. It goes both ways. She knows I'm thirty pounds overweight, but doesn't seem to mind."

Mark raised an eyebrow in contemplation. As if mentioning his weight made him hungry again, Tony eyed the drying triangles of pizza.

"So tell me how it started," Mark asked.

"There's not much to tell. I stopped by a few weeks ago to see Amy, but she was in Fort Erie. Victoria let me in and we started assembling a puzzle."

"A puzzle?"

"Five hundred pieces. I know it sounds stupid. But that's the point: it was nothing major. We only talked, it's just that Amy wasn't there. When I went to leave, she hugged me, and without thinking, I pecked her on the cheek. Reflex more than anything. She invited me to see a movie that weekend. We both assumed Amy would come along, but she was chaperoning a dance, so it was just Victoria and me. At the end of the night, something clicked."

"That's it? That's all you're going to give me?"

"Well, we made love last Thursday. I've been above the clouds since then."

"This is from left field."

"Yeah, I mean, I always thought she was attractive, but she was Amy's roommate."

Tony fell silent, picking up a pizza slice and biting into its point, focusing on the hockey game.

"So?" Mark urged.

"So nothing."

"Does Amy know?"

"Uh-unh."

"Oh man, you've got to break it to her. Especially because of what happened. That should make for some awkward conversation."

Tony swallowed his mouthful. "I'm not sure how to tell her. Amy's trying to pull herself together, but it's been a tough year. It's baby steps for her. Victoria thinks that maybe…"

"What?"

Tony hesitated. "Well, you know I've been looking out for Amy. She's usually by herself at the cottage. Okay, she interacts with people every day at work, but sometimes it's like she's wrapped in heavy-duty cellophane. Because I've been reaching out, making sure she's still connected with the world, Victoria thinks that maybe Amy has developed secret feelings for me. Like I'm some kind of protector or surrogate father figure."

"She had feelings for you last spring. She kissed you."

"Yeah, but that was a one-time thing. A whim. We never acknowledged it."

"Unbelievable," Mark muttered. "You've got two room-mates who are after you, and we're three years past the statute of limitations!"

7

Cazenovia Creek, named for an Indian tribe native to the
region, snakes through several towns in Western New York,
flowing west, north, then west again, eventually emptying
into the Buffalo River, which drains into Lake Erie. Those
who live along the creek are familiar with the perils of flooding. When weather warms, ice topping the frozen creek
stagnates and backs up, cracking with the unpredictability of
a thunderclap. Water below erupts, bubbling over the surface.
Flash floods of this nature may disgorge ice cakes, some as
large as cars, which destroy yards and damage homes.

Due to both proximity and design, one South Buffalo
neighborhood is particularly prone to flooding when mercury
rises. Property there was once marked by wealth and prestige,
largely because of its nearness to Cazenovia Park.

Frederick Law Olmsted, the noted landscape architect,
designed several parks in Buffalo in the 1870s. By the 1890s,
Olmsted had turned his attention to other cities, but his
stepson and partner, John Charles Olmsted, was at the helm
when the family firm was contracted to create parkland in

South Buffalo, which would become known as Cazenovia Park. The terrain selected was a flat, rectangular, seventy-six-acre plot with the bisecting creek that carves the landscape into irregular twists and turns. Olmsted knew the tributary was subject to overflow — his descriptions refer to its "raw, caving banks" — so he attempted to harness that into an asset. The stream was dammed to create a twenty-acre lake dotted with islands. The lake, however, was plagued with problems almost immediately: erosion and siltation led to its abandonment. The dam has been lost to history; the modern park's natural feature is the rugged Cazenovia Creek.

But 19th Century problems remain a central feature of the waterway: it is prone to overflow. At the west end of the park, two-story homes stacked close together on either side of the creek. The flowing water is held in check by giant concrete retaining walls that slope 45 degrees toward the trickle of stream, forming an oversized V-shaped gutter through the dense collection of buildings. Residents who live here are alerted about ice jams and flood watches whenever the creek backs up, usually during spring thaw. Rarely do such cautions occur in February.

On Friday, February 18, 1994, as weather warmed and ice chunks in the creek began to melt, Buffalo Police Officer Daniel Pupo had been assigned the job of patrolling the neighborhood. He was to move slowly up South Legion Drive, use the loudspeaker to encourage people to evacuate, help anyone struggling to get out. The task might be formidable. The area's once elegant homes had turned decrepit with age, now largely composed of elderly and low-income residents. Pupo needed to clear one side of the creek, while across a pair of parallel bridges, fellow officers were performing the same job on North Legion Drive, the opposite bank.

Most homes appeared deserted to Pupo's eyes. In the driveway of a duplex covered in red brick facade, a seventy-something man heaved a duffel bag into a car's trunk. Pupo touched the brakes and called from his open window, "Need any help, sir?"

The old man's voice had thinned with age. In an uneven warble, he replied, "No thanks, officer. I'm going back in to get an extra blanket, then I'm heading to my niece's house in Lackawanna."

"Anyone else inside?" Pupo wondered.

"Just me. Thanks for stopping, but I'll be fine."

"How about your neighbors? Anyone left here that you know of?"

The man's sagging shoulders shrugged. "Far as I know, everyone's gone. Precautions, you know."

Pupo waved and proceeded. Through the rusty cyclone fence that rimmed the basin, icebergs continued to bunch and cluster, tumbling slowly as they floated, propelled by the current below. Pupo studied the retaining wall, noting the uppermost contour line of concrete was hidden by the ice floe. He had used that marker to gauge the water's height just ten minutes earlier. The creek was rising — and fast.

Further down, at the Stevenson Street intersection, three teenagers leaned over the bridge's rail to watch the ice jam chug below. The road had been blocked from traffic with wooden sawhorses, but that did not deter kids from venturing onto its plank. Pupo saw them and thought, if an iceberg collides with the bridge's anchor points, the span could be loosened and washed away. If those kids are on it…

Pupo nosed the patrol car toward the overpass and flipped on his siren for a long moment. The teenagers leaped at the blaring sound. The officer opened the car door, standing to shout, "Come on guys, you need to get off the bridge."

"Aw man, do we have to leave?" a boy in a maroon jacket replied dejectedly. "I've never seen anything like this before."

* * *

Friday, February 18, 1994 | 10:45 a.m.

Since moving to Buffalo from Plano, Texas, nineteen months earlier, Jill Barto's life motto became "school sucks." It wasn't just school that sucked, although that was a big chunk of it. Most everything else sucked too. There was weather, which was cold year round. Even summers were chilly compared to her familiar climate. There was the fact that all her friends still lived in Texas. These northern kids wanted no part of her, dubbing her "Tex" in brash accents that squawked flat and nasally. One of the rockhead jocks taunted her by hissing that the Dallas Cowboys — who had beaten the Buffalo Bills in the last two Super Bowls — sucked monkey balls. As if Jill gave a shit about some dumb sport. The worst thing was that her parents divorced — thus the move back to Western New York, where her mom grew up. Her dad was still in Plano, and Jill didn't know when she would see him again.

In history class, Jill learned the slang for northerners who moved south after the Civil War was "carpetbaggers." She did not know if there was a similar put-down for southerners who came north, but half expected her new classmates to invent one. An ignorant fat kid who sat in the front of the room had called her "wetback," but he was clearly a moron because she was neither Mexican nor illegal. In fact, her skin was pale as polished ivory. Her mom said she was pretty, but

Jill didn't want to be pretty. She wanted to remain anonymous, so she dyed her hair industrial black, painted dark circles around her eyes and wore loose, baggy clothing.

In keeping with the "school sucks" motto, her daily approach was to remain on the fringes of everything. Sit in the corner of the cafeteria. Gravitate towards a wall in each classroom. Don't be first to class, but don't be last either. Don't flunk, but don't ace anything. Simply, she did not want to be noticed. Let me do my thing, don't hassle me, and I'll stay out of your way, she wanted to tell people. It will be a situation to benefit everyone. All through grade nine, Jill succeeded in being an average girl who loathed school.

She was fully prepared to hate sophomore year as well. Actually, most of her classes were bunk. She was at a decrepit campus with decrepit teachers who couldn't cut it in the real world so they chose mediocre professions and wasted their days in classrooms with kids who didn't care. When would she need to use sine, cosine or tangent? She had no plans to be a mathematician. It was all horseshit.

But art class was different. There was a younger teacher, Miss Black, who was cool on several levels. When she talked to Jill, it wasn't to annoy her. There was a reason, a real motivation, for speaking. Usually the topic was a project Jill was working on.

"I see you chose to go with earth tones here," Miss Black said, looking over Jill's shoulder as she brushed a canvas. "Is there a reason you don't want bright colors?"

"They'd contradict the mood," Jill said, pleased by her teacher's compliment, appreciative of a challenge to her artistic judgment.

"All right," the instructor replied. "Just be careful you don't fill that upper corner with too much brown. You'll draw attention away from the entire piece by making that the focal point."

There was a quality about Miss Black. Like Jill, she dressed in oversized clothing and had dark hair. She wasn't really pretty — nor was Jill — but Miss Black could have been, if she made an effort. Maybe a diet and workout regimen. Her cheeks sagged and her eyes were sad. Jill wondered why. There had been rumors last year that Miss Black's father or grandfather or somebody died suddenly, but Jill had not known Miss Black then. Now she wondered if that contributed to her teacher's melancholy.

There was nothing wrong with sadness, Jill believed. Her favorite line from As You Like It, which she read in English, was an ancillary to her motto: "Why, 'tis good to be sad and say nothing." Life generally was sad; the sooner one recognized it, the more bearable it became.

In fact, Jill liked Miss Black enough that she began to consider a career in art herself. Not as an art teacher, not for the world. Deal all day with surly sixteen-year-olds? No thanks. Jill thought about being a real artist, maybe a graphic designer at an advertising agency. Something she could do that kept the creative instincts flowing. When she painted, she felt unburdened, like she was expressing some inner sliver of soul. It was a strange, foreign feeling, and it scared Jill to think she might unwillingly reveal some key part of herself.

Another cool thing about Miss Black was that you could talk to her like a person. She didn't treat you like she was the high and mighty teacher and you were the peon student. She actually took time to listen — you could tell she was sincere.

"Miss Black, do you paint on your own?" Jill asked. "I mean, outside of school?"

"Sure."

"What medium?"

"Mostly acrylics, but sometimes I'll do a watercolor."

"Are you working on something now?"

"Yeah. At my house I have a giant canvas tacked to the wall. I'm trying to paint a specific mood." Miss Black offered a wry smile. "It's hard work creating a masterpiece."

"You should show us some of your work," Jill said. "I'd like to see it."

Miss Black thought for a moment, then nodded. "I could bring my portfolio if you want."

"Really?"

"Stop by Monday. Come in before homeroom and you can check it out," she said, moving to the next table and monitoring students' progress there.

How many teachers would do that? Jill wondered. Most would just blow her off and say, hey kid, don't worry about me. Just take care of your own business. But Miss Black was willing to share. She might be the only thing that made this lousy school worthwhile.

"It's supposed to warm up this weekend," said the freak at Jill's table. "Into the sixties. Bunch of us are going to meet at Delaware Park to play frisbee."

You people have no idea, Jill thought. Like sixties is even warm.

* * *

Friday, February 18, 1994 | 11 p.m. Television newscast
WGRZ-Channel 2-Buffalo

"Kevin, I have a feeling we're going to love this weekend weather warm-up."

"We're in for a balmy Saturday and Sunday, Maryalice,

courtesy of a mass of warm air that's sweeping up from the Gulf of Mexico."

"This could be a rare February day when parents can take the kids out to play without the mittens and scarves."

"Absolutely get the kids outside — walk the dog — whatever you need to do. If you still have scattered leaves in your backyard from October, this could be the time to rake them into piles, but with the warming trend, you're going to be standing on some soggy ground. Let's go to the facts and figures.

"Maryalice, it was a surprisingly warm day today, one of those days where you can almost taste that spring is around the corner, and the good news: it's only going to get better this weekend. You can see we had a high temperature of fifty-six degrees at the airport today. That reading was taken at 5 p.m., and that's the warmest temperature we've seen in Western New York since way back in November. Tomorrow we are expecting much of the same, and I predict the mercury is going to climb past sixty. There is one down side to this, as I hinted at a moment ago. The National Weather Service has issued a flood watch for Erie and the surrounding counties. There is concern about ice jams on local creeks, and that could spell flooding for people who live nearby. Let's go to the Doppler map..."

8

8

Victoria Maxwell had an unusual ability, especially among women her age, to radiate self-confidence to both those who knew her and utter strangers. Looking at her, one would never suspect that she suffered insecurities or inhibitions. She stood at 5'6", but plumb-line posture made people assume she was taller. Her body was lean, athletic; her movements smooth and graceful. To casual observers, Victoria was a remnant of some mythical golden age, where women were always elegant and refined.

Few knew that Victoria's internal feelings opposed that image. She often felt like an outsider. What others interpreted as calmness was muted silence, propelled by nervous fear of failure. Part of it came from living two states away from home. Being 300 miles from her supportive family forced her to make decisions independently, when she would have rather deferred to mom and dad's wisdom.

Nor did she consider herself beautiful. When Victoria saw her reflection, she did not recognize the elegance that others perceived. Hers was a plain face, she thought, smooth but

uninteresting; straight hair was forgettable, a neutral shade
of sand. Half a lifetime ago, during her early teens, boys
at school nicknamed her "spider" because long limbs were
disproportionate to her body. That awkward, gangly teen
still lurked within her frame — she scrutinized its remnants
when she gazed into a mirror. Although no one else knew,
she sensed grotesqueness within herself.

Another factor in Victoria's insecurity was fear of the
unknown: in her first twenty-five years, she had never failed.
Not at school, nor sports, nor her personal life. Concern that
that day might come haunted every decision she made. At
times she considered surrendering, blundering intentionally,
just to get it over with. Before she could really taste life, she
reasoned, she would need to experience a significant mistake
and swallow its unfamiliarity. She suspected its flavor would
sting, biting like unsweetened chocolate.

Victoria had always been successful — in high school she
was an honor roll student and an all-county volleyball player
in Toledo, Ohio. She came to the University at Buffalo on an
athletic scholarship, but after her second year, the women's
volleyball program folded. She considered transferring to
continue the sport, but realized there was no professional
future in that realm. In her first two years in Buffalo, she had
adapted to life away from home, made friends here, was able
to cope with the weather, traffic and the pace of each day. To
transfer now would force her to begin the process anew, and
she was reluctant. When the university agreed to honor her
scholarship for another two years, even without the volleyball
program, that guarantee tipped the scales in favor of staying
put.

But when volleyball evaporated, so did Victoria's single-
minded focus on achievement. Her grades slipped, which

surprised her. Having time away from the gym, she thought, would allow for increased study hours. Her marks fell off the dean's list for the first time (although, to keep perspective, she still maintained a 3.4 GPA) and she found herself spending more time on leisure activities that she had never explored because of volleyball. She regularly watched movies in darkened cinemas, drank lattes in bohemian coffee shops, and let fraternity guys pay for her drinks on weekends. She graduated university, at age twenty-two, history degree in hand. But without a strict regimen of school or sports, Victoria felt lost for the first time, unsure what direction her future should take. Should she teach? Do research? Apply to grad school?

Returning to Toledo was something she considered. Her father, a prominent lawyer, would secure her a job there. But stubbornness seized Victoria — she desired to make it on her own. She leased an apartment with Amy Black, a fellow UB student who she knew peripherally from a poetry class, and found employment with a temp agency. Within six months, she had landed steady work filing and proofreading at an insurance firm. The novelty of her first job excited her: earning a paycheck, living independently far from home. That lasted another year, until tedium began to fill her working days. Victoria found herself watching the clock, anticipating lunch breaks and quitting time.

She needed to consider her future.

* * *

In her final year of high school, Victoria Maxwell's English teacher had been passionate about two things: his impending retirement, and James Wright, one of Ohio's foremost poets.

An aging man whose fashion sense was twenty years out of style, the teacher often read verses from Wright's canon. The poet's eloquent work was direct and simple, evidenced by the line that resonated with Victoria all these years later: "I have wasted my life."

I'm twenty-five, she thought, too young to be paralyzed by inaction. I want all the things that everyone else wants. I want to bask in the American Dream: fall in love, be married, build a career, delight in my children. I want to live in a nice home and splurge on vacations. I want to cook big meals at holidays and special occasions, filling my dining room with the laughter of relatives and friends. I want to be able to lounge in a hammock by a lake and breathe humid summer air beneath a setting sun.

I know what I want, Victoria recognized. But I have no idea how to achieve it. With each passing day my dream feels more slippery, elusive.

"This shouldn't be happening to me," she lamented to her father on the phone. "I was always above average. I graduated top ten in high school, I got a full-ride to UB to play volleyball. Somehow, in the past few years, everything that I earned has slipped away."

"Honey, don't say that," her father consoled.

"It's true, daddy. I have wasted my life."

"You're young, sweetheart. You haven't wasted anything. You're getting your feet under you, and you're doing fine. You've made friends, found a job and you're independent. Your prime is ahead of you, not behind."

"It doesn't feel that way. People my age are getting married, starting families. Mom was twenty-two when I was born. By the time you were my age, you and she were settled."

"It's apples and oranges," he said. "You can't compare yourself to your mother and me. We were a different generation. There were different values and expectations. You're doing fine, honey, I truly believe that."

Unsure, skeptical of her father's reassurance, she took solace in the words of a dead poet.

* * *

Saturday, March 27, 1993 | 10:17 a.m.

"Life is short," the minister spoke calmly from the pulpit. "Life is fragile. We have evidence of that today. Sadly, we do not always know or understand God's will for us during our brief days on earth, nor do we know the exact amount of time we are allotted to live here. Richard Black was a good man, a man who loved and took care of his family. He also took care of himself. He was a jogger, a health food enthusiast. He worked out three times a week and swam laps at the YMCA pool. Although he was sixty-one, to look at him, you would never know it. He was fit and trim. By all accounts, he should have lived longer than he did. And yet we are left to ponder the puzzle of God's will. Why would the Lord, the compassionate, giving, loving God, call Richard Black home now, when he was so meticulous about caring for himself and his loved ones?"

Victoria Maxwell, dressed in a black skirt and blazer, huddled in the small church. Next to her was Tony Davenport. In the first pew, closest to the altar, Amy Black sat with her mother and sister. Faces remained stoic as they assembled to hear the parson's words. Adele Black raised a kerchief to her eyes, dabbing gently.

"But I ask you this," the reverend continued, his voice gaining power as it echoed off pastel walls. "If God gave you the opportunity, today, to be enlightened about the hour and moment of your death, what would you say? Would you choose to know how much time you have left on His earth? And if you did know, would that influence your behavior? What would the world be like if we all knew when and where we would pass into God's kingdom?

"How many of us would grow arrogant by that information? How many of us would procrastinate more than we already do? Why should I help the poor, Lord? I know when I'm going to die, and I have another thirty-six years to help the poor. Today I'm focusing on me for a change. Why should I obey the fourth commandment, Lord? I have another sixty-six years to consider my father and mother! I'll honor them tomorrow.

"Life does not work like that, my friends. And I'm glad the Lord does not share with us the exact hour and moment we will pass into his kingdom. He knows it. He knows it for sure. But by keeping that date a mystery to us, we can appreciate the value of time. We consider today the honorable life that Richard Black lived, and we ask ourselves about our own use of time. With the blessed hours we've been granted, are we doing all we can to honor the Lord? Are we doing all we can to make the world a place where His word can take root and flower?"

* * *

"I bought a book today," Victoria told Amy ten days later. Amy's brow arched in wordless contemplation. Victoria flopped an oversized study guide on the table between them.

The glossy white paperback was titled "Preparing for the LSATs."

"LSATs?" Amy asked. "You're thinking of law school?"

"I've been thinking about a career for a while," Victoria admitted. "The insurance firm just isn't cutting it anymore. It was a good starter job, and I'm glad I've got the work experience, but I'm stagnating. At work today, after lunch, I played a little game with myself to see how long I could go without glancing at the clock. I thought if I kept my eyes averted, before I knew it, quitting time would arrive."

"How'd that go?"

"Horrible. I'd catalog a couple files, convince myself it had been a half hour, and look up at the clock. Once ten minutes had passed, but more often it was only two or three. For a while, I seriously thought that maintenance was repairing the clock from a remote location. It was like time had stopped."

"So you want to be a lawyer?" Victoria moved her mouth with uncertainty. "It would certainly make my dad happy, to follow in his footsteps."

With the mention of Victoria's father, Amy's mind tumbled into somersault. Thirteen days after her father's death, her heart was still raw.

"I thought about teaching, like you," Victoria continued, trying to move her friend from dark reflections. "But I don't know that I'd have the patience. If a kid didn't do something right, I think I'd jump in and do it for him. I thought about trying for a master's in history, but if I don't want to teach, I'm not sure what good that would do me. So I think I'm going to look into law school."

"Law school would be good. I can see you doing that."

Victoria hesitated. "I don't want to say that this is entirely motivated by your dad's death, but I think there might be a lesson here. The minister preached that life is short. I thought about his words and realized I'm not using my time effectively. I've been going through the motions, sort of wasting away my days. My job is like one of those gerbil wheels, where I just keep spinning and spinning without going anywhere. I've been living for the present, not thinking about a long-range plan. I think one of the legacies your dad left is that I'm going to try to be more productive. It's time to seize control of my life."

So shortly before her twenty-sixth birthday, Victoria Maxwell started an upward career path, just as Amy Black began her descent into mourning.

9

"Amy popped in yesterday after school to do some laundry," Victoria Maxwell said. "She asked what I was doing this weekend."

Tony Davenport stroked Victoria's hair. "What did you say?"

"I didn't know what to say. I wanted to say, Tony… I'm doing Tony. But I kind of stumbled around. Studying, I guess. I was non-committal. She probably left thinking I'm some kind of retard. We have to tell her."

"Yeah."

A flickering candle provided the bedroom's only light. From its perch on the dresser, the tiny flame threw elongated shadows against the ceiling. Under a goose down blanket, Tony sprawled on his back. Victoria lay on her side, leg crooked over his knees, body contoured to his frame. Her face nestled in the pocket of flesh between his neck and shoulder.

"I know we aren't doing anything wrong, but it feels like we're illicit lovers sneaking around," Victoria said. "I want to be able to tell her about the greatest first date ever. From now on, that's how I'm going to refer to last Saturday at the Small Boat Harbor."

"Wait a minute. We went on dates before that. What about the volcano movie?"

"I don't want anything to do with that movie. People are going to ask us about our first date fifty years from now. Are we going to bring up the world's worst movie?"

Tony's chest swelled. They had not spoken of the future, but she had just admitted that this relationship was serious enough to project ahead fifty years. He flashed to snapshots accumulated across five decades, imagined colors fading as edges curled from a sticky album. Tony as a seventy-five-year-old man; Victoria his wife for half a century.

"It'll make for a good story," he said.

"No. Walking out of a movie does not make a good story. Walking on water makes a good story."

"It's been done. Ever read the New Testament? Spewing lava, that's where it's at."

"Are you always this argumentative?" she exhaled. "My point is, I think we should take Amy to the harbor."

"Really?"

"Yeah. Let's do that again, only bring her this time."

"Why?"

"Because the ice reminded me I'm alive. I saw the world from a different perspective. Things were familiar, yet it forced me to consider them in a new way. Maybe that's what Amy needs. I don't think it will snap her out of the funk necessarily, but it might kickstart her for the climb back."

"What if she won't go?"

"Then we kidnap her," Victoria deadpanned.

Tony slid from the bed, closing the window. Temperature

had climbed into the fifties earlier, but with night's onset, chilly air seeped in.

Victoria glanced at his bare bottom through the dim. She appreciated his lack of self-consciousness. It's cute that he trusts enough to let me see pouches above his hips, she thought. She repositioned herself against his body when he lay down.

"Okay, I like the concept," he said. "But we need to think bigger."

"Bigger?"

"Widen your horizons. Walking the harbor lasted ten minutes. We could circle around a few times and stretch it to a half hour, but that's about it. I say we try a real adventure."

"Like what?"

"Let's cross the lake."

"The lake?"

"Yeah. Amy's got the cottage in Fort Erie… we could camp there. How far can it be? A couple miles, maybe? We could probably do it in two hours."

"I think it's more than a couple miles."

"I don't know. Where I grew up you can look across and see Canada, so it's not that far. It's not like we could get lost."

"Where did this idea come from?"

"Guys in high school always talked about doing it. Far as I know, no one had the balls."

"Is it safe?"

"Why not? The harbor is safe, right? The lake's been frozen since November. Ice fishermen drive ATVs out there every day. They go so far you can't see them from shore."

"Really?"

"Maybe we could do it tomorrow. The weather is supposed to be warm. We'd have to bundle up, of course, but we wouldn't be shivering the whole way."

Victoria ruminated. Tony sensed her hesitation.

"Should I call Amy?" he asked, hoping Amy's consent would sway Victoria. He reached for the phone on his nightstand.

"She won't be at the apartment. She's having dinner with her mom, then going to the cottage."

Tony dialed that number, speaking into the answering machine: "Hi Aims. I don't know what you're doing tomorrow, but I've got an idea for you and Victoria and me. Call me tonight."

Victoria peeled herself from Tony's shoulder and repositioned on her back. "If she agrees, maybe that's the time to tell her."

"You think?"

"Why not? We'll have a couple hours where it's just the three of us."

"You mean get her onto the middle of Lake Erie, then break the news?"

"Exactly. She won't be able to storm away. She'll be forced to deal with it."

"Tough love."

"It's going to be uncomfortable for all of us. But at least this way, we're confronting the issue head-on instead of tiptoeing around."

Tony agreed, although a part of him romanticized the ongoing deception. So far, Mark was the only one who knew of their tryst. Getting facts into the open would unshackle them, but it would also lend an air of seriousness. Taking the relationship to the next step was a good idea. In addition to coming clean with Amy, he wanted to tell his family.

"I wonder what she thinks about the time we kissed," Tony

said.

Victoria paused. "Who kissed?"

"Amy and me."

Victoria's body stiffened. Her neck craned so she could see Tony's face. "You and Amy kissed?"

Tony watched her pull away, surprised by the reaction. "You didn't know?"

Victoria propped onto an elbow, shoulders angled, and tugged the blanket so it covered her chest. Cool space drifted between them.

"How would I have known?"

Oh shit, Tony panicked. What did I just say?

"I thought she would have told you. Don't girls talk about stuff like that with their roommate?"

"When did this happen?"

"I don't know... last year. Right before her dad died."

"Right before her dad died?"

"A couple days before. We were both a little drunk. It happened once, and we never talked about it. End of story."

"Oh my God. How did I not know this?"

"I don't know. I thought you did."

She remained on the far side of the bed. Space between them seemed to grow. Her tone changed to annoyance. "How would I know?"

"As I said, I thought Amy would have told you."

"No, Tony, she didn't tell me," Victoria snapped.

"Okay, I get that. I'm sorry."

"You're sorry? How do you think I feel?"

I have no idea how you feel, Tony thought. But I sense it's not good.

"Did you make love to her?" Victoria wondered.

"What? No, of course not. Victoria, it was a kiss. It lasted maybe thirty seconds. It happened once. That was it. It didn't mean anything. It's not like I'm in love with her."

"I don't believe this." She stared at him, bewildered by his blank expression.

Victoria's mind sputtered into tangents. She considered Tony Davenport. Who was this man? Handsome, with a boyish smile, spilling hair and a bit too much flesh padding his cheeks. They had known each other for three years, that was true, but how much did she really know? What other secrets did he possess? Were there hidden tales of lost love, broken engagements, something as sinister as jail time? What stories muddied Tony's past?

"Do you understand why I should feel upset?" she asked.

He inhaled so air filled the sides of his lungs. "Not really."

"Not really? Are you kidding me? I just make love to you to find out during pillow talk that you made out with my roommate!"

"A year ago."

"The roommate you've been spending all your free time with until we hooked up last week."

"Because her dad died." Tony waved a hand to punctuate his words. "I've been spending time with her because she's depressed. You don't think I'm in love with her, do you?" Victoria folded arms to shut out such thoughts. "Now I don't know."

"Come on, Victoria. You can't mean that."

"This is a... a... shock," she stammered. She turned her back to him, spiraling into the sheet and sliding from the bed. She padded down the hallway, bare feet tacking against the hardwood floor.

Tony stared at the ceiling. Although saliva puddled in his mouth, his throat turned to sandpaper. He had difficulty swallowing.

At the far end of the hall, Victoria flipped on the bathroom light, shut the door and squinted into the mirror. She adjusted disheveled hair, reflection blurring as tears welled. The room was stuffy, confining. She dabbed the pinch of her eyes with a tissue, then slid the window open, resting her cheek against its molding, cool air spreading like a noxious vapor.

10

Adele Black studied her daughter over the rim of a steaming teacup before tilting it toward her lips.

"You should know I went on a date," she said nonchalantly.

Amy had been scanning this month's Good Housekeeping which was open across her mother's kitchen table. Slow to react, she looked up, cocking her head and narrowing eyes. "You what?" she asked skeptically.

Between them steeped tea in a ceramic kettle, its pot-bellied sides twisting with indigo vines and heart-shaped flowers in a jungle pattern. Heat radiated from within, repelling mother and daughter to opposite sides of the oval table.

"I went on a date. I didn't think it was a big deal, but your sister thought otherwise. She said you wouldn't be happy about it."

"You went on a date?" Amy repeated. "With a man?"

"Of course with a man. What do you think?"

Amy noticed age lines flanking her mother's eyes. Recent stress had etched them into deepening canyons, splayed in

wings toward her temples. Adele's hair was thinner than
Amy remembered. Naturally dulling to gray, her mother had
changed to a subtle hue of reddish blonde. Between strands
of russet glowed the pinkish flesh of her scalp. She was older
than Amy liked to consider.

Confused, Amy wondered, "Who did you go on a date
with?"

"Jason Barnswell."

The name stung against her cheek. Comfort collapsed,
like a building imploding. Amy bubbled with hot tar.

"Jason Barnswell? Two doors down?"

Adele nodded. "I know you and your sister never cared for
him, but he's really quite a nice man."

"Mom, he's a creep. Being near him is like red ants crawl-
ing up my back."

"Have you ever spoken with him?"

"I tried to avoid speaking with him for years." Amy
paused. "Isn't he married?"

"His wife left him a while ago."

"She smartened up, eh?"

"Amy!" Adele scolded. "That's no way to talk."

Jason Barnswell was the neighborhood oddball. In a manner that needed little description, he was weird — and so
was his family. He was obsessive about his yard. During her
teens, Amy was aware of Mr. Barnswell trimming the lawn
without a shirt, pouchy stomach and flabby breasts jiggling
as he sputtered along on a riding mower. Thinning hair was
combed across the scalp, but while cutting grass it drooped
off one side, like a sagging dishtowel. While his pate was
balding, a bramble sprang from his back and stomach. He
had an unsettling, nervous, giggly laugh that sounded por-
nographic. Walk by his house on a July night when he stood

shirtless and hunched over, edging blades of grass away from his concrete driveway. "Hi Amy," he would say, in a baritone whisper. "Heh, heh, heh." It was enough to cause Amy's jaw to tighten.

Barnswell's only daughter, Marcie, was a social outcast at school. In grade seven, Amy had tried to befriend the girl, but she was aloof, uninterested in a relationship. Perpetually dressed in black, Marcie clumped through the school halls wearing heavy combat boots. Stringy hair covered much of her face; what little flesh remained visible was riddled with acne.

"Marcie always had zits," Amy told her mother accusingly.

"So what?" Adele asked. "Does that mean I can't speak to Jason, because his daughter had acne ten years ago? Your complexion wasn't always clear either. That's part of being a teenager."

"You really went on a date with him? Where did you go?"

Adele raised the teacup to her lips. She held a mouthful longer than necessary. "He took me to dinner. It was no biggie, but I enjoyed myself enough that I asked him out again."

"You asked him out?" Amy spat. "Are you losing your mind?"

"No, dear, I'm not. But I'm lonely."

Adele Black had never been comfortable alone. As a child, she used to leave the snugness of her own bed and creep into her sister's room to sleep on the floor, just to be near someone. When she grew old enough that a babysitter was no longer warranted, Adele made sure a friend was with her when her parents ventured out. Being alone frightened her, left her vulnerable and unsettled. During her married years, when Richard was at work, aloneness was never an issue — she reveled in the company of her children. When they began school, Adele worked part-time as a restaurant hostess, synchronizing the shift so her hours ended with the school bus' afternoon drop. Now in her fifties, Adele still dreaded solitude. Losing her husband was enough of a shock; the fact that it left her alone in an empty home was a second blow.

"Lonely or not, I don't know how you can do this to dad," Amy said coolly. "It's selfish."

"How do you mean?"

"You know damn well how I mean," she said. Her rising voice was shaky, unstable. "You're thinking of yourself and no one else. Dad's not dead a year, and already you're soiling his memory by going out with a creepy neighbor? If he was here, he would be as repulsed as I am now!"

Hurt stabbed deep in Adele's eyes. I will not give in to this, she thought. I will not sink to her level. She struggled to keep her voice calm. "Amy, I love you, and I loved your dad, but you're out of line!"

"I'm out of line? I'm out of line? Oh, that's just great!" Amy wavered now, anger radiating. She pushed back her chair, standing suddenly. "Hollywood couldn't write comedy like this! The body isn't even cold in the casket, you're off with the sleazy neighbor, and I'm out of line? This just sickens me!"

Adele raised her voice now too, trying to match Amy with decibels. "Well you're going to have to get used to it! I've got another thirty years on this planet, and I'm not going to spend them alone! It's too hard! I can still love and deserve to be loved back!"

* * *

The cottage across the river had been in the Black family

since the 1940s, when her grandfather returned from World War II and purchased lakefront land. Ten minutes from the Peace Bridge, it had been Amy's summer home through her teenage years. Even when she was old enough to work a seasonal job, she gladly commuted to Fort Erie when her shift ended.

Old growth pines surrounded the house, wooden exterior darkened by age, fallen needles and cones matting the driveway and patchy lawn. Viewed from the kitchen window, the inlet of Crescent Beach lay flat, interrupted by protruding rocks near shore. Across Lake Erie crouched the southern fringe of Buffalo.

Nestling at the cottage seemed a smart idea last autumn. Her mom and sister would not venture near — too many memories of Amy's father, they whined. Most neighborhood residents were part-time, so with winter's approach, Amy found solitude. Within its sanctuary, she could lock the door, pull curtains, and close out the world.

Since her father's death, Amy's nighttime dreams became a swirling palette of childhood memories. Images bled together from the suburban split-level in which she grew up. In one dream, the family was painting its whitewashed siding on a sweltering July day, taking turns with rollers and brushes; in another, Amy was ten again, dressing dolls in the sunken family room. Sometimes she could smell syrup and pancakes wafting from the kitchen; water-smoothed grit calloused her hands while she constructed gravel dams in the creek behind the house. Amy and her sister scoured the shore, plucking indigo and purple flowers, wading into current to overturn broken shale slabs and uncover crawfish. When she sputtered awake and grogginess passed, Amy wondered if there was some psychological explanation for her dreams — in this time of uncertainty, mourning her father, did the subconscious revert to safe images of childhood, where her world was immune to heartache?

Amy's method of dealing with grief had always been to paint. Her father bought her a cheap plastic tray of water-colors before she attended kindergarten. More than twenty years later, she still valued it as the most thoughtful gift she ever received. It allowed her to express complex feelings, emotions she could not put into words, and unwittingly pushed her toward a career.

At the cottage, Amy unfurled a giant six-foot tapestry to serve as a square canvas. Tacked to the wall, she rearranged furniture for easy access. Tubes of paint and brushes were arrayed on a table's edge like a surgeon's operating equipment.

The swatch would be filled as an abstract monument to her father. Colors, textures and values she chose would reflect his life of generosity, his commitment to family. Amy would conquer anguish by capturing the man's essence on canvas.

Yet she had no idea how to begin.

For weeks she stared at a blank muslin sheet, confounded. This stalemate was uncharacteristic. She earned a bachelor's degree in fine arts. The basement at her mother's house was littered with colored canvases mapping her growth from child to adult. Painting had always been natural, motion and energy rather than pre-planning. Why was this so hard? Sentimentality? The imperative to get it right?

Amy enjoyed teaching because students lacked inhibition. Give a kid a brush and paints, and within seconds, they are slapping color down without fear of screwing up. What is the worst thing that can happen? Amy prodded the rare kid who turned reluctant. Do something you don't expect? Big deal. You can cover it up.

Now, Amy longed to be so carefree. Her task was daunting enough that she felt paralyzed.

11

Tony Davenport wasn't sure what had happened two hours earlier — how things had turned so ugly so quickly. Replaying the conversation in his mind provided little analysis. It was an innocuous comment, muttered without forethought, and suddenly the evening tilted toward disaster. Victoria had returned from the bathroom with shoulder-shaking sniffles. In wordless conviction, she dressed and left Tony's apartment.

Tony felt like an ass. How could he have expected Victoria did not know Amy kissed him? How could he have predicted her garish reaction?

He phoned Victoria's apartment every few minutes, but if she was home, she did not answer. He kept leaving messages.

"Victoria, I'm sorry. Please don't be mad. I'm crazy about you and you know it."

This entailed risk. He knew Amy planned to spend the night in Fort Erie, but if by some fluke change of plans, she heard the messages before Victoria, their secret would be exposed. That would only compound the situation. It was a calculated gamble, but making amends with Victoria was more important.

Now he hoped Victoria was on the other end of his ringing phone.

"Hello?" he said anxiously, then braced when he heard Amy's voice.

"Hey Tone. I got your message."

He exhaled. "Are you at the cottage?"

"Yeah, I just went fifteen rounds with my mother. Wait until you hear this…" She recounted her mom's date with Jason Barnswell. "And then, to make things worse, I got stuck in traffic on the bridge. There's never any traffic at 11 o'clock on a Friday. I wanted to paint tonight, but I'm too upset. I'd just make a mess of things."

"Relax," Tony said. "You're home now. You can decompress." He wanted to share his foibles, talk about Victoria storming from his bedroom. Frustration burrowed into his stomach, yet he had no outlet. That conversation would have to wait until he and Victoria revealed themselves.

"Yeah, I'll take it easy," Amy agreed. "The message said you wanted to do something tomorrow?"

Tony sold the idea of leaving from Hamburg Beach, hiking across the lake and camping at the cottage tomorrow night. He feared the last part might be a deal breaker. She had turned reclusive — no one besides Amy had been inside those walls for months, so he was surprised when she readily agreed.

"Sounds good," she said. "You're sure it's safe?"

"Absolutely. It's going to be warm, but I'll probably call the Coast Guard before we go, just to see how thick the ice is. That will reassure Victoria too."

They planned for Tony to cross into Fort Erie and pick

up Amy at 11. They would come back to meet Victoria at Hamburg Beach, where Tony and Victoria would leave their cars parked overnight. Sunday morning, after spending the night at the cottage, Amy could drive them back.

Tony hung up the phone, wondering if Victoria would even make the hike.

* * *

After leaving another message on Victoria's machine, Tony dialed Mark, who answered on the second ring.

"What are you doing?" Tony wondered.

"Sitting here in front of the tube. I was supposed to meet Poochy for a beer, but he never called back. So tonight it's me and Jay Leno."

"You're watching Leno now? Last time we talked you were pining for Carson."

"This guy's no Johnny, but I can't fight NBC. What are you up to?"

"I'm in a bind, man. I just had my first fight with Victoria."

Tony braced himself. He suspected that Mark would gloat, chant I told you so, dish off some yarn about how it was just a matter of time and that all women were feeble and moody.

But Mark said only, "Tell me."

...So the evening was relaxed... Victoria and I were enjoying witty banter... She was into the idea of trekking across Lake Erie... we hatched a plan to spring our news on Amy... But then, I stupidly opened my mouth... Swallowed not just my foot but the entire leg...

When Tony finished, Mark said, "I guess there aren't billboards advertising it, but how could she not know?"

"That's what I thought. I figured girls talk about that stuff."

"So now she's pissed at you."

"Seems like an understatement."

"Hmm," Mark contemplated. "She'll have to calm down, right? I mean, five minutes earlier she was talking about how you needed a good first date story to tell in fifty years. So this is a blip on the screen."

"You think?"

"Absolutely."

The words were soothing. Tony wanted to lap them, taste their coolness and swish them around his mouth. But a pang of doubt flicked his front teeth. Look who I'm talking to, he thought. Could I find anyone who knows less about women?

"Anyway, you want to come with us tomorrow?" Tony asked.

"Not if you and Victoria are going to tell Amy. I'm no fourth wheel."

"It could be moot. Who knows if Victoria is even going to go? She may not want to date me anymore, so there won't be any news to break."

"Well, anyway, I can't," Mark said. "I promised my mom I'd help her clean the basement."

"C'mon. That can't wait?"

"You want me to say no to my mother? Are you crazy? You know how obsessive the woman gets when she cleans! Cockroaches in the next county get nervous."

"Yeah, all right. Maybe we'll grab a bite on Monday or Tuesday?"

"Sure."

"Hey Mark? Thanks."

"No worries. Next time we talk, you and Vicky Max will

probably be planning a wedding."

* * *

Buffalo News: Saturday, February 19, 1994. Front page.
(morning edition only on Saturdays)

BALMY TEMPS TO REMAIN
IN WNY THROUGH WEEKEND

Check the calendar.

Yes, it is still February, but you might not know by looking outside.

Friday's temperature of 56 degrees was the highest local reading since November. The National Weather Service forecast suggests that today the mercury could soar above 60 degrees.

"We may see a record high for the date on Saturday," said meteorologist Steve Chudzik of the National Weather Service. "It's going to be close. This warmup stems from an air mass originating in the Gulf of Mexico. It's sweeping northward and could keep us unseasonably warm through Sunday."

While high temperatures have lured many people out of their homes, the good news comes at a cost: the National Weather Service has issued an ice jam flood watch for Erie and surrounding counties.

Residents in South Buffalo and West Seneca who live adjacent to Cazenovia Creek have been evacuated as a precaution. By nightfall, as temperatures cooled, the creek appeared to have crested. But expected warmth may keep residents from their homes for another few days.

The Erie County Sheriff's Department is issuing cautions

as well: continuing balmy temperatures and an easterly wind could spell bad news for ice fisherman.

"I would not venture onto any sort of frozen surface this weekend," warned Capt. David McClusky of the Erie County Sheriff's Department, after taking a helicopter survey of Lake Erie. "This could be a disaster for people who go on the ice."

If cracks open close to shore, McClusky warned, fishermen could find themselves trapped, cut off from land.

"With warm sun melting from above and currents moving below, it's just not safe to be on the lake this weekend," McClusky said. "From the helicopter, I saw about two dozen ice fishermen riding ATVs near Sturgeon Point. I urge everyone to use common sense and stay on land for the next few days."

Sunday's weather should remain in the 60s, but by Monday, temperatures are expected to drop back down to the 30s.

12

When Captain David McClusky touched the wall switch, fluorescent lights sputtered to life, a flickering harsh yellow glow as the lecture hall illuminated. He stood surrounded by the sunken stage, near a lectern, tapping toes nervously against tile flooring. Above him, curved rows of desks were bolted to ascending platforms, amphitheatre style. Shaped like a crescent moon, the sterile room's tiered seating reminded McClusky of terraced farms in South America.

McClusky stepped to the podium and rested his hands on its faux wood edges. He flipped the microphone on, exhaled into its head, a fuzzy amplified echo bouncing against the far wall. He adjusted the foam cover so its malleable stem aligned with his mouth. Despite the room's emptiness, a fluttering jabbed his stomach's pit.

McClusky did not enjoy teaching. He was a helicopter pilot, not a professor. Anticipation created unfamiliar nervousness. He had led seminars before and knew that once initial awkwardness was overcome, he performed well enough in front of a crowd. But anxiety that preceded a workshop was gnawing, uncomfortable. Sleep had been fitful the night before. He dozed for ten minutes at a stretch then readjusted his body beneath sheets. At 2 a.m., Molly had had enough. "You're on the couch, buddy," she hissed. "I've got to get up in the morning too, you know." As he stumbled from the room, she slurred without moving her lips, "You'll be fine tomorrow, honey. Relax."

His wife's reassurance did not soothe him last night, nor did recollection offer comfort now. McClusky unloaded the cardboard box of materials, assembling them in an orderly line on a folding table beneath the chalkboard: overhead transparencies, rope, cold water survival suits. Nothing to worry about here. This is all familiar.

His daughter was the teacher, not him. Megan worked with seventh graders every day, leading them in rudimentary science experiments. He admired the way she could engage a roomful of thirteen-year-olds. She had provided tips to begin a lesson: "These are adults, so open with some lighthearted banter. A joke maybe. Get them on your side. State your objectives clearly, and dive right into material. You know your stuff, and they'll sense it right away. Be sure to monitor their interest. Nothing's worse than some guy rambling on who has no idea that he's lost the audience."

Megan's advice was good, and McClusky was confident about the topic he presented. He was an expert on cold water rescues. Now forty-seven, he had been on the job for a quarter century. He had plucked people from the brink of Niagara Falls — troubled souls who waded into the river intent on suicide, then, deafened by the roar of a 176-foot drop, had a change of heart and found themselves unable to turn back. He had pulled ice fishermen from the cracking surface of Lake Erie — sometimes the same people more than once.

Between rivers, creeks, gorges and the lake, Erie County had eighty miles of shoreline. McClusky was familiar with nearly all of it.

Several years ago, the chief had approached McClusky with the idea that trainees could benefit from his experience. It took arm-twisting, persistence and even a hard sell by his wife. "Part of the reason you joined the department was to rescue others," Molly reminded him. "Running a seminar is just another avenue to doing that." She was convincing, as usual, and she was right. Now, to calm his jitters, he reminded himself of the big picture — the purpose was to save lives. Just be cool, McClusky repeated to himself as a mantra. I've done this before. There's no need to get worked up.

A door opened in the back of the lecture hall. A skinny guy with a brush cut — he couldn't have been more than twenty — peered in nervously.

"This the seminar on ice rescues?" he asked.

"This is it," McClusky replied. Seeing this kid barely old enough to shave, knowing this was the personification of trainees, McClusky's stomach dipped all over again.

* * *

"The first thing you need to know is that you are not a superhero. You're not Rambo. You are a human being and you are just as vulnerable — sometimes more so — than the person you are trying to rescue. A good law enforcement aviator has the word 'no' in his vocabulary. If you're at a point where you're going to go beyond your personal limits or the limits of the helicopter, you are putting your life in jeopardy, your partner's life in jeopardy, the victim's life in jeopardy, and you might very well ruin a two-million dollar helicopter.

Raise your hand if you want to be on the hook when that bill comes in."

McClusky watched as the collection of young faces chuckled.

"I've been with the department for twenty-five years, in charge of the helicopter team for the last fourteen. In that time, I've made more than 300 rescues. In the past twelve months alone, we've rescued twenty-two people. Some of the rescues are quite dramatic; others are fairly ordinary. None of them are ever easy, because you're responsible for another person's life. That's never something to take for granted. I'd like to say that we've saved everyone, but I can't. People have died on my watch, and that's a feeling I never want to get used to."

The thirteen fresh-faced young men and women studied their notebooks solemnly. A few heads bobbed in agreement. In the time it took to say these words, McClusky had won them over with his commanding presence. Thin and wiry, he stood taller than his six-foot frame. His face had no visible delineation of chin. Instead, cheeks narrowed toward his neck like a crinkled fleshy funnel; salt and pepper hair drew attention away from the absent jawline with a halo of dignity. The man was firmly in control of this lecture hall.

Nervousness evaporated as he clicked on the overhead lamp, directing attention to the projection screen.

"First, a definition: drowning is death due to asphyxia caused by immersion in fluid. Usually that fluid is water. It is estimated that about 140,000 drowning deaths occur each year throughout the world. In the United States, approximately 6,500 drowning deaths happen annually. Most victims are children or adolescent males. After car accidents, drowning is the second leading cause of injury or death for children under fourteen. In general, males are more likely to drown than females. There is no definitive reason why, but I theorize it's due to more high-risk behavior. In this country, a majority of drowning deaths are related to swimming, but other frequent causes are boating, scuba mishaps or accidents involving motor vehicles.

"Most drownings occur when a victim passes out or is too exhausted to access air. Examples might be a swimmer who has a heart attack and is unable to continue; a person who breaks through the surface of a frozen lake and experiences exhaustion then coma caused by hypothermia. It could even be a drunk passing out in a puddle. You could drown in a few centimeters of water if you're face down. Sometimes adverse weather conditions cause drowning, like high waves that knock a person off balance, or riptides or current shifts like you see on Baywatch."

The young faces grinned at McClusky's pop culture reference. When he asked who was a fan of the cheesy TV show, most males raised their hands (one muttered "Pam Anderson is smokin'!") while the females, a minority in this seminar, furrowed brows and shook heads with exaggerated disdain.

"The initial reaction to submersion has a big, fancy technical name," McClusky continued. "It's called the Mammalian Diving Reflex. Has anyone ever heard of that?"
Blank expressions indicated they did not, so McClusky explained that when a body is submerged in water, it automatically shifts into energy saving mode. The phenomenon occurs in all mammals, including marine animals like seals and whales. Triggered when the face comes in contact with water, the reaction is a method of maximizing survival time in extreme conditions.

"There are several factors to the Mammalian Diving Reflex in humans: heart rate can be reduced up to fifty percent; breathing becomes inhibited; blood flow to extremities is reduced while pumping increases to vital organs, especially the brain, heart and lungs. During deep dives, when pressure is higher, blood shifts to the chest and neck to prevent collapsing lungs. Overall, the reflex is sharper in young people. It is because of these reactions that a person can survive longer without oxygen underwater than on land, even if unconscious."

A burly trainee with a goatee and dark sideburns raised a hand. "The Mammalian Diving Reflex only happens when your face gets wet?" he asked.

"Yeah, isn't that odd? It's like there are sensors in your face that create a reaction. In fact, anytime you go swimming, the Mammalian Diving Reflex begins. The effect is more severe when water is colder, but it happens anyway, regardless of water temperature. When you swim in seventy- degree water, your normal body temperature of ninety-eight point six degrees actually cools off. Nature is trying to level out the disparity and reach a steady median. If you stayed in seventy-degree water long enough, eventually, your body would cool to that temperature."

McClusky paused, looking at the young man's sideburns. "Good question." The trainee nodded thanks.

"So what happens during submersion? If conscious, a person will hold his breath and try to find air. If he can't get air, chances are he will begin to panic. As you might imagine, the rapid body movement which ensues burns valuable oxygen in the bloodstream and speeds up the time leading to unconsciousness. The official name for inadequate oxygen in your blood is hypoxia.

"Think back to high school biology: oxygen in blood is

used by cells, which convert it to carbon dioxide. So as the level of oxygen decreases, the amount of carbon dioxide increases. Higher levels of CO_2 create a stronger breathing reflex. The more CO_2 in your blood, the more urgent it is that you inhale to replace missing oxygen. Divers call this time at which a person can no longer hold his breath the 'breath-hold breakpoint.' When the breakpoint occurs depends on several factors, such as the individual's size, weight and fitness. It can be increased through training.

"You should know that there are two different types of drowning: wet and dry. Unfortunately, they have the same outcome." McClusky paused, expecting a stray chuckle, but was met with silence. He continued, undaunted. "When water enters a person's airway, the reaction is to cough or swallow. If underwater when this occurs, both reactions lead to more water intake. A human throat will naturally constrict, sealing its air tube, preventing water from entering the lungs. Water that does get through is diverted into the stomach. The scientific name is laryngospasm. The positive is that a person's lungs are free of water. The negative is that not much oxygen gets through either. A small number of people can maintain this seal even after passing out. In death, no water has entered the lungs, so this is considered a dry drowning. In eight-five to ninety percent of people, laryngospasm will relax after unconsciousness, and water will flood the lungs. This is wet drowning. What's interesting is that TV medical shows profess that water in the lungs indicates a victim was alive during drowning. That's true. But absence of water in the lungs could mean the same thing if a dry drowning has occurred.

"The heart stops beating when there is lack of oxygen, or chemical changes take place in the lungs. Clinically, this is cardiac arrest and the victim is dead. However, there could still be a chance of rescue. The brain cannot survive long without oxygen — on average, six minutes is the limit. But, if immersed in cold water, metabolism slows down — thanks to the Mammalian Diving Reflex. There is a documented case of a child surviving after being submerged in cold water for an hour and ten minutes! Another eighteen-year-old male lasted for thirty-eight minutes underwater! It's rare as hell, but it can happen. The lesson here is we are very reluctant to give up on a rescue.

"These are the facts surrounding drowning." McClusky paused for effect. "Which of you is going to tell me I'm a poet and don't know it?" More smiles from the audience. "Next we need to discuss facts about ice safety and look at the body's reaction time to being submerged in cold water."

13

Tony Davenport woke like a sloth, thick-bellied and lethargic. His body felt like it had slow-roasted overnight. Stumbling to the bathroom, he checked the thermometer mounted outside the window. Temperature was already in the low fifties, which explained why he felt overheated under winter blankets.

The good news was that Victoria still planned to make the hike. The bad news — plenty of it — was that Tony heard this from Amy, who called as he was eating breakfast. Victoria still had not returned his messages or answered the three calls he placed this morning. She had not spoken to him since storming from his apartment. Tony remained confused about her reaction. Did she not understand how crazy he was about her? How could kissing Amy a year ago even matter now?

Their first five seconds together would tell him much of what he wanted to know. Her body language would project any petulance. He planned to be direct: sorry to have offended, insist that he made an innocent confession, without malice. It happened that Amy kissed me a year ago, it was a fact, so let's accept it, not let it come between these feelings we have, and move on. You're the focus of my life now. It's not Amy. It was never Amy.

Tony did not think to retrieve the Buffalo News in his paperbox before leaving to pick up Amy.

* * *

Saturday, February 19, 1994 | 11:56 a.m.

Gazing westward from Hamburg beach, the view was as raw and primitive as the dawn of creation. Canada loomed across the expanse of Lake Erie's horizon like a shadowy strap of worn leather. Treelines were too distant to be distinct, yet when sun reflected across the pale expanse of ice, an optical illusion tricked the eyes. Miles of space diminished so ridges of the far shore felt close enough to touch. One could stretch a hand to span the vastness.

At the edge of beach, ice chunks nestled against the tundra of frozen land. Straight ahead, almost due west, the Canadian shoreline turned sharply and disappeared behind itself, so that to the left, nothing was visible except the opaque hues of whitened ice and sky. Pivoting right, buildings in downtown Buffalo clustered against each other, poised to spring skyward. The truss of the Peace Bridge crouched in the distance.

Tony Davenport and Amy Black stood on the snowswept beach staring across the glaze towards Canada. Both wore sweaters and jeans. Amy was dressed in a knit cap and a green sleeveless down-feather vest with gloves tucked into the pockets. That morning, she had not been sure what to wear, musing whether it was too warm for a jacket. Better to have ample clothing than not enough, she decided. In her left pocket were two granola bars and an eight-ounce plastic water bottle.

Tony wore black wayfarers, but had forgotten his baseball cap. Its bill would have shielded his brow, but that was a minor inconvenience. As usual, he spent little time considering wardrobe — instead, he felt anxious. Too many subplots were happening here, tremors which rattled his foundation. He checked his watch, glancing toward the road behind him.

"She's always late, you know."

Amy remained unmoved. "You don't have to tell me," she replied.

Amy did not sense his nervousness. She had withdrawn into herself, studying the lake. Warmth had cracked winter into a gentler shape. Air smelled innocent, like the breath of angels. One did not have to stare long at this expanse to find goodness in the day. God's creation, she thought. I'm lucky enough to share it with friends.

She was transfixed by pastel values — giant watercolor brushstrokes that bled into one another. Trained as a painter, she appreciated chromatics, but the interest was more than simply colors. Since childhood, her mind had assumed the need for structure. Varying shades here could all be explained by atmospheric conditions. There was a purpose to the manner in which things occurred. Science had proven that. For every action, there is an equal and opposite reaction. Cause and effect. Order. Logic. Her father's death had changed that belief. No one could explain why the jack slipped and her dad was crushed. Amy no longer understood the reasoning behind life's events. She considered that there might be a bitter randomness, a silent soaring chaos, which prevailed in the world. It was a disturbing thought, one that she could not yet disprove. Perhaps truth lay hidden along the horizon.

Accumulated snowdrifts were polished white, shiny and sparkling. Not far from shore, dunes tapered away, exposing a mix of blue ice and mud colored snow. Further out, the hue faded dull, and imperceptibly bled into sky. Moving her eye upward, the heavens darkened to a rich indigo, punctuated by creamy clouds. It was orderly and just, the way nature should be. Amy wondered if she could somehow capture this scene on a canvas.

"Look this way and tell me what colors you see," she said, pointing.

Tony turned toward the lake. He had been raised a few blocks inland, spending hundreds of days on this beach as a child. Now he lowered plastic sunglasses as if witnessing the panorama for the first time. "White... with a hint of blue, I guess," he said slowly, sliding glasses back up his nose.

"That's it," Amy agreed. "White and blue. That's all you can see. Subtle shades of those two colors. Nothing else on the spectrum."

Tony checked his watch and glanced toward Route 5, anxious that each passing car might be Victoria's Oldsmobile entering the parking lot. Impatience brewed. Why is she always late? he thought. What will her mood be?

"Do you know that white, by definition, is the absence of color? I learned that as a kid. Black is a combination of all the colors. My dad used to say there was a little bit of everything good in me, and our last name proved it."

Tony turned toward Amy. "Your dad was a wise man."

She kept her eyes straight ahead. "I know. I miss that wisdom. I wish I could shake away the hurt."

Tony paused respectfully. "I'm sorry, Aims."

She forced a weak smile. "I know I don't say it, but I appreciate everything you've done. You've helped me more than anybody. You're a bright light in my life. I just wish I wasn't an albatross around your neck all the time."

"You're not an albatross."

"I feel more comfortable with you than anyone else. My sister and I never got along, so she's been no help. And my mom is off dating. Uggh," she croaked. "The thought makes me physically ill. Even Victoria — I mean, I love her, but, sometimes she's so focused on law school that she doesn't really understand my need to feel sad."

"Is it getting any easier?" Tony wondered.

Amy noticed hopefulness on his face. He was an optimist, a trait that defined his character. Light snuck behind the lenses of his sunglasses, where she witnessed genuine concern. Tony's hair was windblown and tousled. Stubble poked from the curve of his chin. He was boyish, charming, and so sincere. "It's always easier when I'm with you," she smiled. "And I'm making an effort to find something good in each day."

Tony felt a vest of responsibility heaving onto his shoulders. Was she beginning to unlock emotions? Was this a warm-up to confessions of love? Amy admitted she felt better with him. He could not reciprocate those feelings, not when Victoria had wrapped a stranglehold on his heart.

A beeping horn pierced the moment. Victoria's white Oldsmobile crested the hill, moving down the incline and to the gravel lot. Tony's stomach tightened as he watched the car come to a stop. Here we go, he thought.

Pushing up a sleeve, he checked his watch. "She's only five minutes late," he said.

"That's like being fifteen minutes early for her," Amy

muttered. "We must be making progress."

"I'm going to toss this pair of gloves in her backseat," Tony said quickly, displaying them like evidence before trotting up the incline. He wanted to speak to Victoria privately, without Amy's listening ears, even if the conversation was brief. When he reached its plateau, Victoria opened the car door and stood. She wore jeans and an oversized Buffalo Bills sweatshirt, adjusting a backpack across her shoulders. She pulled sandy tresses thoughtlessly into a ponytail.

"Hi," he said, landing a meek kiss on her cheek. He chose a kiss to gauge her temperament. If she turned toward him, or smiled, or offered her lips, things were going to be okay. If she stiffened or drew away, tension would thrust between them.
Victoria accepted the kiss stoically, without reaction. Tony was unsure how to interpret this. Amy, on the frozen shore below, had her back to them as she studied the lake.

"I'm sorry I upset you," he said in a low voice. "I didn't mean to."

"I know. I heard your messages. I didn't feel up to calling you back."

He shook his head dismissively.

"In a way it's good the truth came out," she said. "Better now than six months or a year from now."

He breathed deeply. "We going to be okay?"

"I don't know." She slid a knit cap over her head, tucking ears under its edge. He waited for her to say more, but no words came.

"Victoria, you're important to me. This," he waved his hand in the space between them, "is important to me. I don't want it all to go away over something that truly meant nothing."

She remained distant, unconvinced. "Okay."

"I'd like to talk to Amy. Tell her how we feel."

Victoria looked across the Oldsmobile's hood toward her roommate, who stood facing Canada like a jade carving, hands in pockets.

"Right now I'm not sure what I feel. I'm just trying to get through the next few hours."

Get through the next few hours? Tony thought. What the heck is happening? But he chose to not push this. Not here. Not yet.

"Fair enough," he said.

Tony and Victoria descended the hill. He wanted to take her hand or wrap an arm around her shoulder — anything to be connected — but felt timid, tentative. Victoria would not want that now. Amy turned as their crunching boots approached.

"Is this weather amazing, or what?" she asked. "You picked the perfect day."

"Let's hit it," Tony said, clapping his hands. "If we leave now and keep a steady pace, we should be at the cottage no later than 3:30 or 4."

* * *

At 12:09 p.m., with mercury creeping above 60 degrees, the three left shore from Hamburg Beach to begin the slow trek across Lake Erie in a northwest direction. At their point of departure, ice was clear and windblown smooth, nearly a foot and a half thick. Below, thirty-two-degree water churned in a slow current.

Each carried a different concern at departure.

14

Victoria Maxwell did not like cemeteries, and never had. Perhaps her phobia stemmed from horror movies she and her friends watched on Friday nights during middle school — dark, grainy films on late-night TV in which tombstones rumbled over, earth splintered open, and albino zombies in tattered clothes pried themselves from rotting coffins to terrorize unsuspecting innocents. During teenage sleepovers, after the movies had ended and the TV flickered to snow, Victoria and her friends would remain awake until dawn's approach because turning out lights was simply not an option after seeing such absurd horrors.

Those silly middle school nights were a dozen years past. There was no reason to be nervous in a cemetery on a sunny, cool May afternoon. Still, Victoria reflected, offering to accompany Amy here had seemed like a better idea last night when sitting in the comfort of their living room.

Memorial Day was for remembering the dead. Two months had passed since Richard Black died. This was not a military thing. Amy simply wanted to place a flag on his grave. It would be her first visit there since the interment.

Sprawled on the couch, Victoria thought for a few moments. Returning to the burial site would be hard for Amy. She would not ask her mother along because of their constant bickering. Nor would Amy seek out her sister. She would make this visit solo. Victoria sensed the impending loneliness, the hollowness her friend would experience the next day.

"If you want, Aimer, I'll come with you," Victoria offered, stifling her phobia.

Now, beneath the spanning limbs of shade trees, Victoria stood by Amy's side before the austere tombstone. Its grey polished granite shone new, a contrast to surrounding headstones, which time had weathered a darker hue. Beneath an arcing upper edge, "Black" was etched in long, thin letters, a cross flanking each end of the surname. At the bottom of the squared base, Richard was labeled "father," with birth and death dates. Victoria became unsettled when she noticed "Amy, daughter," carved adjacent to her dad.

Sunlight felt refreshing against the warming air. Victoria could taste summer on her lips. Despite this, Amy had withdrawn mutely into herself, arms folded across her chest as if chilled.

"It's a nice stone," Victoria said, wondering if her words sounded empty. "But Aimer? Why are you being buried next to him? Shouldn't that space be for your mom?"

"Ugh. Don't get me started," Amy lamented, looking away from the tomb. "The crazy woman wants to be cremated. She wouldn't hear of reserving a plot for her. Said it was too morbid to think about."

"It is, a little," Victoria said. "You shouldn't be worrying about your burial site when you're only twenty-eight."

Amy's eyes remained sad, returning to the grave. "Going to happen to all of us eventually, right? Death and taxes."

Yeah, Victoria thought sarcastically. Coming here was a really great idea. She did not mention the possibility that Amy might someday wish to be buried next to her own husband.

Victoria laid tulips at the grave, and Amy propped a miniature American flag into the ground close to her dad's name. Victoria nodded silently to her friend and stepped back.

Three rows over, a white-haired man in jeans and a denim vest walked with a plastic watering can, splashing potted geraniums that nestled between graves. The open hatch of his van loomed on the narrow access road.

Splintering slowly from Amy, Victoria chose a path away from both Amy and the groundskeeper. Branches from a pine tree were cut high enough that she did not have to duck under them. Their fist-sized cones peppered the lawn. Rather than vertical headstones, some of the older graves — people who had been born in the 19th Century — were marked with flat shale laid in the soil. Grass encroached corners of these markers and spilled over top, needing to be edged lest it obliterate names.

And what names they were, Victoria noticed. This section of the cemetery hosted a regular Irish wake. Ambling through parallel rows, surnames echoed with the old country's rolling hills of green. Courtney. Sullivan. Burke. McCarthy. Connery. McGroder. Doyle. Carey. Victoria knew that South Buffalo had been predominantly Irish-Catholic, but until now she never realized how expansive that population had been.

All these names... generations of people with their own stories. Who, for instance, was Charles Leary? The tomb-

stone before her revealed he was born in 1898, and lived until
1972. Victoria wondered what he had looked like when he
was her age. Tall with flaxen hair bleached by summer sun?
Broad shouldered, with a mole on the left side of his neck?
How did he court Susanna, the wife buried adjacent to him?
Was their romance memorable to anyone but them? How
did he earn a living? What did their children and grandchil-
dren remember of them? Are there still pictures of Charles
and Susanna stuffed in a photo album, edges curling, colors
fading to brown?

It's just like Spoon River Anthology here, Victoria
thought. Thousands of dead, people like Amy and me, with
lives that long ago were important and unique. Today, who
remembers? She hesitated, breaking stride. Maybe, she considered, if I listen closely, I can hear their stories, like water
lapping against the shore's edge.

The cliché is that cemeteries are silent. Be quiet and
respectful of the dead, people are told. Silence was a myth.
Wind shook oak branches, camouflaged birds clattered in
leafy limbs, engines hummed on the road beyond wrought-
iron fencing. Victoria thought of the old joke: why do cemeteries have fences? Because people are dying to get in!

She zigzagged up a row and pivoted back toward Amy,
who was anchored with shoulders hunched, transfixed before
her father's grave. The moment was serene, but Victoria
chose to interrupt. A person mourning can drown in too
much solace, she thought. There was something just a little
too eerie about this entire place.

15

"Any rescue situation on ice has to be considered extremely dangerous," Captain David McClusky explained to the class. "You need to take every precaution that you can. One mistake, and boom, you're in the water too. Now you are no longer making the rescue, but you're a victim who needs to be rescued. There are signs which give clues when ice becomes unsafe to walk on, but too often those signs are not clear to a novice. Sometimes, in spite of all the training we can provide, ice strength is disguised, so the first evidence of weakness is when it collapses."

McClusky had the attention of thirteen trainees before him. In the past hour, he had garnered respect for the group. They were young, naïve and starry eyed, a bit too quiet for his liking. He preferred active learners, students who peppered him with questions. But the baker's dozen was focused, absorbing his words, jotting on notebook paper, bright, eager faces fixed on him at all times.

He placed a new transparency on the overhead. "Here are some facts about ice: first, clear ice is stronger than ice which is cloudy or discolored. Newer ice is also stronger. The longer a cover has been there, the more opportunity for weakness, from both the sun's rays above and currents below. Ice around obstructions — things like rocks, pilings, docks — has the potential to be weak. Uneven depths cause different melting and freezing patterns. Ice strength depends on several factors including air temperature, water temperature, water depth, thickness, snow cover, currents. If ice is less than four inches thick, it's probably not strong enough to support more than one person.

"When you are involved in a cold water rescue operation, the best rule to follow can be summed up in two words: be prepared. Yes, you are in a hurry. You've got a victim in the frigid water, and you need to move fast. But take the extra time to prepare yourself. That means wearing thick clothes, like wool, in layers. Limit skin exposure as much as possible, and monitor yourself and your colleagues for things like frostbite and hypothermia. Have spare dry clothes nearby. Wear hats and hoods. If you have access to a heated area close to the rescue scene, use it! Take breaks and let a partner relieve you. A successful rescue begins with thorough preparation.

"There are so many hazards you could face, depending on the situation. At a cold-water rescue, you could be dealing with rough terrain, rocky shores, steep embankments. All of these things hinder your abilities. There are times when you have a limited access area, so boats and maybe even the helicopter aren't going to be useful. If you're vulnerable to wind chills, frostbite or hypothermia, that's going to complicate the rescue."

McClusky replaced the transparency on the overhead with a chart that chronicled the body's reaction to drops in core temperature.

"The human body reacts strongly to temperature changes. We all know that your average core temperature is ninety-eight-point-six degrees. It varies slightly for every person. When that temperature begins to fall, even just a few degrees, to ninety-six, it can cause shivering or teeth chattering. Drop further to between ninety-five and ninety degrees, now you're getting into intense shivering, almost convulsions. At this point, a victim would struggle to speak. Keep going down: between ninety and eighty-six degrees, muscles become rigid, movements turn jerky, comprehension is dulled. The person isn't thinking clearly, but at a rudimentary level, he is still aware of where he is. It's not until eight-five to eighty-one degrees when the victim becomes irrational. He loses contact with his environment, drifting into a stupor. Pulse and breathing are slowed, muscles are rigid, and this is the time when cardiac arrhythmia — irregular heartbeat — may occur. By eighty degrees, falling into the seventies, most people will lose consciousness and their reflexes will no longer function."

A hand was raised — the same burly kid with goatee and sideburns who had spoken earlier. McClusky pointed to him.

"How will we know the victim's temperature?" he wondered.

"You won't know exactly, but you'll be able to estimate from their behavior," McClusky replied, thankful for a break in the monotonous drone of his own voice. "If you arrive at a rescue scene, you should be able to judge whether the victim is lucid or not. You'll be able to estimate how long they have been submerged and know the urgency of the time frame you're dealing with."

"Is there anything a victim can do to preserve body heat

if they are in the water and we can't get to them right away?" the trainee asked.

"That's a great question," McClusky said, again placing a new transparency onto the projector. "It leads into our next section. There are three main areas of the body where heat loss occurs: head, groin and armpits." McClusky pointed to each area on himself as he spoke, and demonstrated the motions as he explained each. "There are ways to reduce heat loss in each area. On the head, wear a hat — but something that wraps all the way around your hair, like a knit cap or even a swatch of cloth. A baseball cap isn't going to be nearly as effective because only the top of your head is covered. For the armpit, keep elbows tight against the chest to prevent exposure under your shoulders. To maintain warmth in the groin, press thighs together and bend your waist into a fetal position so that area is closed off.

"Now, how much of this will help a victim is going to depend on the situation. If you arrive at a scene where a guy is stuck in a gorge but is in control of his faculties, then you can tell him how to conserve warmth until he's rescued. If you arrive at a lake where a victim has been submerged in frigid water for twenty minutes, that person is going to be too irrational to follow any instructions you might give. So all of you are going to have to assess the situation and use your judgment about the best course of action to follow.

"How long can a person be expected to survive in water? Well, that depends on several factors, like age, weight, size, the amount of clothing covering skin. Younger and older people are generally at the outside edges of the spectrum and are affected worse. Fact is, people tolerate cold at different levels, but here is a general chart."

McClusky placed the following table on the overhead

projector:

Expected Survival Times:

Water Temperature:	Unconsciousness:	Survival Time:
32	less than 15 min.	15-45 min
33-40	15-30 min	30-90 min
40-50	30-60 min	1-3 hours
50-60	1-2 hours	1-6 hours
60-70	2-7 hours	2-40 hours
70-80	3-12 hours	3 hours-indefinite
80+	indefinite	indefinite

Trainees squinted towards it, copying it into the notebooks. McClusky stopped speaking to give them time. When it appeared most were finished, he continued.

"If there is more than one victim in a cold water rescue, they should huddle together if possible. This helps preserve body warmth and has been proven to increase survival time by up to fifty percent. Whatever the situation, you should always be trying to calm the victim. Reassure them that you're working hard to solve the problem."

McClusky clicked off the projector and stepped from behind the podium. He approached the lowest tier of desks and leaned against one's edge.

"General rule of thumb for citizens concerning ice: unless you're absolutely sure, stay off. Even then, reconsider. Creeks are dangerous because current flow rots from underneath. People think, it's a creek, it's not that deep. If I break through, I can still get myself out. But unless you're sure of the water depth, that's not always the case.

"Lake Erie is the worst. Ice fishermen go out all the time on ATVs, convinced they're safe. I've never had a problem, one guy told me. Maybe he didn't, but I could give you a long list of names from fishermen that I've rescued over the years. Snowmobilers, too. They see this big sheet of polished snow and think it's a playground. They don't realize that if their machine comes anywhere near a weak spot, it's lights out. Five years ago, two snowmobilers drowned near Fort Erie. I spent a day in the air trying to locate the bodies. How's this for dumb? One time from the helicopter I saw two guys fishing from their car about four miles out. Doors were wide open and the heater was cranking. They both had holes to fish through on either side. In the backseat they had a case of beer that was chilling naturally."

Students chuckled in disbelief. McClusky paused to shake his head. "Morons like this survive, then convince all their friends that the lake isn't dangerous. But let me tell you something I believe after doing this job for twenty-five years: it's never safe to go onto the lake. It's too unpredict-able. I don't care how cold it is — so many things could go wrong. I've been preaching this for years, but people still refuse to listen. So I need you, as the next generation of law enforcement officers, to spread the word and help me on my crusade."

16

Victoria Maxwell felt dizzy. The past few weeks with Tony had been the whirlwind she had always dreamed about. She was a child who has just learned the wonder of balance, now skating straight ahead. With Tony's revelation, an obstacle suddenly thrust into her path. Lacking grace, she skidded sideways, puncturing the dreamy bliss. For the rest of the evening, thinking was an array of warped senses. She lay on the couch, studying the ceiling, hoping to regain equilibrium. Knees turned to warm cream cheese when she stood. She could not fathom how both Tony and Amy had neglected to tell her about their intimacy.

Tony was contrite, insisting there was no reason to be hurt. But it felt like he was brushing the incident away, an inconvenient piece of lint clinging to an otherwise glittery overcoat. With anyone else, Victoria would have thanked him for a nice time and walked. But she did not want to. Tony was different. Very swiftly — frighteningly so, as she reconsidered now — he had absorbed into her heart.

She had dated before. Past guys ran the gamut from pleasant to laugh-out-loud. Some were nice to spend an evening with; others were good conversationalists; a few could be labeled alternative bad boys. The feeling, as she described it to Amy after each date, was "tangible temporary." The thought of marrying any of them was outrageous.

Tony, however, was not a passing whim. There was a wholeness to him. Being together felt natural, unforced. After a few weeks, she already considered their future. This was a man with whom she could spend her life.

On Friday night, she was tumbling, unsure how to right herself. Ribs ached and the couch cushions felt squishy. Any other time, she would share lamentations with Amy, but that was not an option here. Irony tasted bitter: she and Tony had deceived Amy, now Amy's past was haunting her. Karma at its cruelest.

Every few minutes the phone rang, and Tony's voice pleaded on its tape.

"Victoria, I'm sorry. Please don't be mad. I should have told you earlier, but I swear to God, I thought you knew. I didn't mean to upset you. Please call me so we can work this out."

After the fifth call, Victoria turned down the volume on the phone's speaker.

* * *

Saturday, February 19, 1994 | 12:09 p.m.

When Victoria ascended giant snow dunes at the water's edge, her boots sunk imperceptibly through the crusted surface. She gasped — a mixture of shock and paranoia — momentarily frozen in place, afraid that moving further would cause the entire hill to crumble and collapse beneath her. Ice formed a base eighteen inches thick, she knew that, and this dune, atop it, stretched at least six feet higher. Logic dictated there was no way she could break through — and even if she did, this was beachfront. Water here was only a few inches deep. She could trudge her way out, feet soaking wet. But sinking two inches left her apprehensive nonetheless.

To Victoria, this was all so foreign, so unfamiliar. Like the relationship with Tony, she had no idea what to do next. Uncomfortable as it might be, she had chosen to honor this commitment to hike Lake Erie. It was the proper thing, but if a law professor cross-examined, she would have difficulty defending the choice. Part of it was the larger implication: two people's plans hinged on her, and neither would hike in her absence. But Victoria also knew that a full day of sitting home and brooding would infect her with leprosy. Walking with Tony and Amy would be a way to confront demons draping her shoulders. She would be uncomfortable, but immersed in her trouble, not keeping it beyond the swing of an arm. By nightfall she hoped to have a clearer handle on this whirling chaos.

She wanted to see two things. First, after a day of close scrutiny, there could be no evidence that Tony still carried feelings toward Amy. Victoria had observed them together before, but never in this context, with the knowledge she now had. How would he respond to Amy's sly smiles? If she touched his arm flirtatiously, would he stop her or revel in the attention? Could he brush away hushed words of affection? How could Tony explain that Amy's feelings had to end, suddenly and permanently?

The second thing was that Tony needed to make Victoria feel safe. He had been apologetic on the phone — that was expected. But could he sidetrack Amy and simultaneously create nurturing space for Victoria? He needed to demonstrate his love, not simply talk about it.

That led to a thorny question: how would Amy react to knowing that Tony loved Victoria now? If they confessed it to her, would they still be welcome at the cottage? In a larger sense, would they be accepted in her life?

Lifting boots and stepping again, Victoria watched Tony on the downside of a dune, chunky frame plodding further lakeward, pointing out tire tracks where ATVs had launched from shore. Dark hair spilled over his collar, wide shoulders swaying rhythmically with his gait. Who is this man? she thought. What do I really know about him?

A harsh screech, like a child in pain, interrupted her ruminations. Tony followed Victoria's gaze. "Look," he pointed.

A solitary crow, ruffled with unkempt feathers, perched atop a light pole in the parking lot with ochre eyes staring downward. It made a rough "caw" sound, hooting as if expecting a response.

To Amy, the sound pierced like a shotgun blast. "A rook! Where did that come from?"

"I don't like crows," Victoria told her friends, reaching flattened ice and venturing further onto the lake. "They're dirty scavengers. Go on, get out of here!" she yelled, flailing arms at the stoic bird. It started back mutely.

"It's our conscience," Tony said. "It's watching us."

"It reminds me of my dad," Amy said. "He loved blackbirds, especially red-winged blackbirds. Said they were our cousins. Check out the feathers on that thing. Jet black, like an oil spill. Black like my name."

"Maybe it's not our conscience," Tony said. "Maybe it's your dad's spirit, watching over us."

"Maybe it's both," Amy offered.

"You guys are freaking me out," Victoria said. "Do you think this is a sign we should turn back?"

"No, no, no," Tony said. He gripped Victoria's hand and pulled her forward. "No backing out now."

She allowed his touch, the first since the previous evening, their only contact past his revelation. Through her gloves his flattened palm was powerful, soothing. The connection reassured her, conveying sincerity. His expression remained serious, eyes boring toward her, hoping to relay an unspoken message.

Victoria pivoted toward the lake, making tentative strides. She was not ready to provide relief for Tony. Still, she thought, he just made a good first effort.

The crow screeched short bursts, like a hyena's cackle, as the three continued walking.

* * *

Ten minutes from shore, already the sound of cars along Route 5 had faded to distant echo. Victoria turned to look back. The crow kept its silent vigil, rumpled ebony feathers a contrast to clear sky. There was the town park building, white clapboard sides reflecting above spindled pilings. To the right, curving behind trees and folding against itself, ragged cliffs dropped from the highway's ridge. She had been too close to notice those when they began the hike.

Beside her, Tony and Amy had fallen silent. The only sound was the muted clumping of rubber soles. Victoria's jitters about the ice had faded now, just as nervousness evaporated after a few minutes of walking the week before. Yet her emotions remained guarded. Tony's silence complicated her feelings.

Victoria paused to adjust her canvas backpack. Looped over both shoulders, it contained clean underwear and socks, a toothbrush and toothpaste. Tucked inside the flap was a letter she had penned to Tony the night before. Its blue ink was an outlet for her spilling rage, but even as she wrote with fury, she wondered if Tony should read it. One of Mark Jablonski's dating rules was "Never put anything in writing… it will come back to bite you." Victoria regarded Mark as a goofball, but thought that rule contained some virtue.

She had folded the letter into an envelope, creased length-wise, and stuffed it within a plastic baggie where she kept a stock of Q-tips. Tonight, when they arrived at Amy's camp, she might give the letter to Tony. Should he be allowed to taste her bitter words, Victoria wondered, or would that only further complicate things?

* * *

Saturday, February 19, 1994 | 1:33 p.m.

"It's farther than it appears," Amy said, pushing a sleeve back to check her watch. "We've been walking an hour and a half and when you look at Canada, it doesn't seem like we're any closer."

"True," Tony agreed. "But turn around and look back."

Each paused to pivot. The American shore had dimin-ished, although it remained closer than their destination. None could estimate with accuracy how far they had come, nor did they know they had unintentionally veered west-ward. Hamburg Beach was a receding white dimple. The abandoned Bethlehem Steel plant, whose angled roofs and cylindrical smoke stacks blackened like a smudge of soot, dominated the azimuth toward land. Clinging to shore along Route 5, reflections glistened from moving cars. Their engines could not be heard this far. The only sound was soothing, windblown nothingness.

Before them, reality had turned primitive: a stark winter vista, opaque and pale blue marbled with hints of turquoise. From shore the path to Canada had looked smooth. But as they trekked further, terrain evolved into something jagged, raw. Ice that had appeared flat was anything but — frozen collisions had caused geological upheavals of giant chunks. Miniature mountains thrust skyward with polished shapes, twenty and thirty feet high.

Such "shoves" are formed when the edge of an ice sheet is adjacent to open water. Wind or eddies bubble waves onto the plain, where it freezes incrementally, adding to the whole like a child packing snowballs. When temperatures plunge, the mass freezes quickly, sharp and pointed like crinkled tinfoil. The shove may grow into a craggy peak, waves splashing additional layers, then become sculpted into odd contours by sun, wind and melting.

"From shore, all we saw was blue and white," Amy observed. "But the further we go, the more the ice turns green, almost like a faded jade. Have you guys noticed?"

"I'm not a color wheel," Tony said. "I don't have the artists' eye that you do. Actually, I think I might be color blind."

"Is that why your clothes never match?" Amy teased.

Victoria sprang alert. Amy was flirting, but was Tony perceptive enough to catch on? Would he squelch this?

"I'm ignoring you," Tony answered lightly, altering direction toward a ten-foot high shove and scaling its incline. "It's like walking on the surface of the moon." He reached the apex, stabbing an imaginary flagpole into its highest point. "I claim this ice for Victoria Maxwell and Amy Black."

Rather than climb the ridge, Amy circled around it. "Look!" she called from the windward side. "There's an opening here. Like a cave."

Victoria followed her into a shallow cavity while Tony scrambled down the side to join them. The hollow was wide at the base, narrowing as it grew taller, and its height was enough for two people to stand comfortably inside. Victoria touched the tips of her gloves against its polished sides.

"This is like a playground," Amy offered. "You could slide down the outside and hide in here. If I were a kid, I'd love this."

"I love it now," Tony said, peering into the opening.

"That's because you're a big kid," Amy told him. She stepped out to allow him space to enter, tousling his un-kempt hair as she passed. The contact — and Amy's half-smile — caused Tony's neck to stiffen. He felt uncomfort-able, especially in view of Victoria. Amy was not a toucher. There was an unfamiliar sparkle in her eyes. Is she flirting, he wondered, or has it been so long since I've seen her smile that I'm just not accustomed to it?

"Come on," Victoria snapped, annoyance wrapped around her voice. She brushed past Tony before he could enter the cavern. "We better keep moving."

17

Skies were pale blue and sun reflected off ice. From the cockpit, Capt. David McClusky and Senior Tactical Flight Officer Danny Vargas could see the jagged, irregular shoreline stretching from Hamburg Beach south toward the county limit. Brightness was so intense that both squinted through their aviator sunglasses.

As part of routine patrol, McClusky piloted Sky One south, toward Sturgeon Point, a popular ice fishing spot in the town of Evans. Despite public warnings to avoid the lake, he knew warmth would lure fishermen to the bay.

True enough, beyond the treeline a scattering of shrunken dots peppered across the smoothness, each hovering over a round opening. From above, they were irregular polka dots.

"Will you look at this," he said to Vargas. "There must be two dozen morons down there."

As the helicopter drew nearer, fishing poles sharpened into focus. The fishermen looked like elves waiting for bread to pop from a toaster. A few turned, pointed, and waved when they heard the whirling chopper blades.

"Hey, nice to see you too," McClusky muttered. "Frigging half-brains."

"I'm surprised that you're surprised," Vargas replied.

McClusky shook his head impatiently. "Radio in to get a patrol car out here and get these idiots off the ice. I can't believe one of them hasn't gone in yet. We'll make a pass up toward the river and then sweep back to be sure they're clear."

"Want to wait here a few minutes? Could be a matter of time before we do a rescue today."

* * *

Saturday, February 19, 1994 | 1:46 p.m.

"Is everything okay with you two?" Amy Black asked.

Victoria Maxwell clenched as if an instrument scraped enamel from her teeth. She halted outside the cavern, turning to face the question. "Why would you say that?"

"You haven't said anything to Tony all day. You're both so quiet. I'm sensing tension."

Tony Davenport looked to Amy, then Victoria. Her expression remained hardened, closed to him. His heart quickened. He did not know the proper thing to say, but was tired of unspoken innuendo.

"Maybe we need to have a pow wow," he told Victoria. "Amy, could you give us a couple minutes alone? You're right — there's tension. Let us talk here in the cave, and after that, we'll explain everything."

Amy donned a questioning look. When it became clear neither Tony nor Victoria would say more, she nodded. "I'll be over here," she said, pointing vaguely toward the distance.

"If sound carries, I'll hear everything you say."

Boot treads faded as Amy moved away. When she was several hundred yards from them, Victoria asked in a harsh whisper, "So it's going to be like this, hmm? You're just going to put it all out here. Pull back the sheet, confess to Amy without consulting me. The hell with consequences, right?"

"Telling her was your idea. It was a good one."

"That was before."

"We've got to get straight, Victoria. How deep are you going to let this get? I'm telling you, it was nothing."

Her tongue felt thick, like she was trying to master unfamiliar sounds of a new language. "I don't…" she started, stopped, then stuttered again. "It's just that… I know I'm overreacting, but I can't help it."

"Talk to me. Tell me what you're feeling."

In a flash, anger exploded. Her voice raised as words rushed back. "Goddamn it, Tony. You don't know?"

"I know you're upset and I understand it. But you're moping around here like a scolded kid. I'm sorry, but I can only say it so many times. You've got to give me something back. Tell me what you think."

"You know what I think. Why am I hearing about this now? Why didn't you tell me before we slept together?"

Wearied, Tony rested his head against the icy cavern wall. "I thought you knew."

"Amy never told me. There's a reason."

"Yeah. Her dad died a few days later."

"No. During the time in between, she could have told me." Victoria stabbed the air with her finger. "Why didn't she? We've always told each other about our dates and what guys we liked. Did she shut me out because she sensed some attraction between us?"

Tony started to speak, then shrugged his shoulders. "I can't speak for her, but I doubt it. You're over-thinking this. It's probably some simple explanation. Hell, you were away the weekend it happened. Maybe when you got back she was out grocery shopping or something, and you were asleep when she came home. I really don't know why she didn't say anything. Let's ask her. But does it matter? Does it lessen the feelings we have for each other?"

"Okay, why didn't you tell me?"

"I did."

"No, before last night. When it happened."

Tony paused, considering the question. "You're projecting our relationship now onto the relationship we had then. You and I never talked about things like that. Not until a few weeks ago. We never hung out; we certainly never discussed romance. We were only friends through Amy. I have no idea who you've dated in the past year, and frankly, I don't care. All I know is that I'm crazy about you. It's time for this fight to end. I want the world to know that I'm in love with you. I want to start by telling Amy."

18

Saturday, February 19, 1994 | 2:31 p.m.

Amy Black stood alone on Lake Erie, one arm folded across her stomach, the other propped so its hand cupped her chin. She rested weight on one hip and crooked a leg impatiently. Low tones spanned the ice, but sound slurred, so she could not decipher words. She was puzzled. Were her friends planning to confront her? Was this some type of intervention? Why were they disagreeing so hotly?

After a few long minutes, Tony Davenport and Victoria Maxwell stepped from behind the shove and began to approach. They were holding hands. This surprised Amy. Victoria appeared ill at ease.

"So here's the way it is," Tony said, as they stopped six feet from Amy. "Victoria and I began dating a few weeks ago. We're in love."

"Oh my," Amy said simply.

She studied both faces, unsure if this was a joke. Both remained impassive. Half-moon pouches below her lids projected a puppy-dog sadness. She felt tired, overwhelmed.

The words slammed her chest. Amy did not betray emotion, but her heart plunged downward, where she felt it rumbling against bony knees. Her mind twisted into a vortex of psychedelic colors. Tony and Victoria? How could it be? And yet here they were, clasping palms before her, professing a misplaced love, romance that belonged elsewhere. Her two best friends — a roommate and a man who had been her rock during the past year…

"Aimer, we wanted to tell you because…" Tony's explanation began. Words continued, a steady, machine-gun burst of clipped sentences, but Amy could not focus. Her mind was a symphony of clashing sounds — cymbals crashing, screeching violins, a cacophony that filled her head and rattled its echo deep into her cortex.

Amy raised a palm to Tony, hoping to subdue the din. "Hold it. I'm stunned — truly I am. I need a minute. I just need a minute." Amy feathered hair back from her forehead, tucking stray locks beneath the rim of her knit cap. She pressed thumbs into temples to alleviate the pounding. Retracing their path, she wandered toward the shove and its sheltered cavern, each step feeling as though it would never end.

Still as an ice carving, Tony and Victoria remained hand in hand.

There is no way this ends well, Tony thought.

* * *

Since her father's death, Amy felt under siege. Friends, acquaintances and strangers all scrutinized her, seeking evidence of mourning. Amy never considered whether the phenomenon was real or imagined. To her, people behaved differently when she entered a room. Some turned serious;

most were reluctant to crack jokes. Friends grew timid, afraid to utter the wrong thing for fear it might trigger a reaction. There were two exceptions: her students, who were cheerfully self-absorbed teenagers, and Tony, who allowed Amy to be herself, without passing judgment. This was the reason she could open her heart to him.

She recalled an evening last winter when they cooked dinner at his apartment. Pots steamed over oven burners; Tony lifted lids to stir. The scent of garlic filled the tiny kitchen. Slicing vegetables, she chattered, unfolding memories.

"When I was a little girl we played this game," Amy said. "My dad would pick me up and wrap a blanket over my head — real loose. I could still breathe but I couldn't see anything. Then he'd spin me around and walk all through the house, and I had to guess which room we were in. It was silly, stupid really. But I was close to my dad, close enough that I could smell his musky scent. His big arms around me were warm and he cradled me against his chest. I was nestled in this cocoon of safety where no one could hurt me. I've never felt so safe. I remember how sad I was when he told me I was too big to play that game anymore. I was eight or nine, and by then I was too heavy for him to carry from room to room."

Amy's voice sputtered. "I'm missing something that I haven't done for twenty years. It's too much, him being gone. Nobody will ever love me like my dad."

"Every girl's first love is her father," Tony said. "It won't be exactly the same, but you will experience love again."

Now his affections fell on Victoria.

Where does that leave me? Amy thought. Is there enough room in his life for both of us? Will I be the perpetual third wheel?

Then, suddenly: how was I not aware? How long have I been

oblivious? How thick are my defenses that I did not suspect this was happening?

Ducking into the shove's opening, shielded from the peering gaze of Tony and Victoria, her lower lip quivered. Tears beaded behind rheumy eyes. Amy looked at the barren plain before her, windswept and smooth. Opaqueness and absence of color mocked her.

First I lost my dad. Now I'll lose Tony and Victoria. For me, there will be no one.

Shortly Victoria appeared, mouth creased with concern, angling her head so she could see into the cavern.

"Can I come in?" Victoria asked.

Amy did not respond to that question, but squeaked "Congratulations," trying to contain tears before they dribbled onto her cheeks. Against her will, her voice sounded feeble. Victoria would not be duped by false sincerity, and Amy knew it.

"You're upset," Victoria said gently, stepping close to rest an arm across her roommate's shoulder. Amy bristled at the touch, but Victoria did not pull away.

"No, I'm not, really. I'm just a little taken aback. Since my dad died, I've been so damn emotional." A tear leaked from the corner of her eye. She massaged it quickly into her flesh.

"I didn't know that you two were… that you and he had kissed," Victoria said. "No one told me until last night."

What was that? Amy thought. An apology? If so, it was halfhearted, useless. "That was a long time ago."

"Aimer, I love him. I'm pissed off right now, but I really love him."

"Good. Good for you."

Victoria removed her arm from Amy's shoulder and hugged herself. "I'd feel better," she said, "if I could believe you when you say that."

"What do you want me to say, Victoria? It's great. It's wonderful. It's everything I ever hoped would happen. I just didn't expect it to be you. You two as a couple was not even on my radar screen. Tony is a generous, caring person. So are you. So it really is a great match. I'm just shocked, that's all. Shocked and emotional."

Victoria studied air bubbles trapped within the contoured ice. In the open, under the sun's rays, temperature was pleasant, but cold felt constricting within the cavern's walls.

"Do you love him, Amy?"

Amy's mind was a battered kite.

"Of course. I love you both."

"That's not what I mean. I mean, are you in love with him?"

Amy hesitated, muscles beneath her jaw twisting into unfamiliar shapes.

"If he and I are going to make this work, I need to know," Victoria said. "Friendship is one thing. Romance is another. I suspected you had feelings for Tony, but I thought it was one of those crushes-from-a-distance that would always be that way. I never knew you kissed."

"Would knowing that have changed anything?" Amy asked.

"I don't know. Maybe. Knowing was never a luxury that I had." After a pause: "So? Do you love him?"

An hour ago Amy might have admitted attraction, but not now. Not in Victoria's company. Doing so would impale her pride. She would suffer this, donning a false face and offering congratulations, trying to sound sincere. Self-misery would be repressed for now. But later, when they reached the cottage and she was able to shut her bedroom door, lie on the bed and inhale familiar musty air, she would revisit sorrow.

"I love him. But I'm not in love with him." Amy turned to look at Victoria. "Does that make it easier for you?"

Victoria scoffed. "Since last night nothing has been easy. But I never intended to hurt you. I'm sorry that your feelings are being bounced around. You have to know I never wanted that."

"Okay, fair enough. But Victoria? This is all so fresh. I'll need time. Time to process this."

"You're not mad, are you? Please don't hate us."

Hate is a strong word, Amy thought. Hate is a venomous, powerful emotion, raw as a Jackson Pollack splattering. She hated what had happened to her father. She hated that her life felt like oozing pus. But hate a person? Hate two friends for declaring their love?

"Of course not."

Hate was not the right word. Bulldozed. Steamrolled. Flabbergasted. But not hate.

* * *

Tony paced behind the shove, awkward as a first-time father in the delivery room. Strains of muted conversation leaked out, but he deciphered tones, not words. He felt like his future was being decided and he was curiously removed, powerless to alter its course. In spite of his bravado by confronting Amy a few minutes ago, Tony had turned timid. He remained in place, afraid to round the corner and join their discussion. The girls need to work this out, he thought. If they come to agreement, contentment will trickle down on all of us.

19

Silence hovering between them was a wounded gorilla. The girls had reached resolution in the cavern, Tony Davenport knew, but he did not hear what was said, and neither volunteered contents of their discussion. Both became curiously mute when they resumed the hike. He had expected the opposite. Tony, reluctant to appear as bumbling fool, followed suit, marching in silence. He was hungry and tired, ready for a nap at the cottage. The goal today was to relieve tension, Tony thought. Mission not accomplished.

Mind still brewing with complexities, Amy Black considered perspective. She instructed students to analyze a subject from different angles to achieve fuller understanding. Her emotions were at war with themselves. Did the change in her relationship with Victoria and Tony necessarily need to be negative? Over time, could she overcome this burden?

There is so much bad in the world, so much hurt and uncertainty. If my two closest friends have discovered a bond, we should celebrate it, because connections don't come often enough. In those rare moments when attraction descends from heaven, its flavors should be exalted, savored, sung from mountaintops.

Then she thought, I don't want this to be the death of my heart. But right now it feels that way.

Canada drew into focus. Trees soared above rooflines of clustered cottages; graffiti spots on concrete retaining walls were blurs of color. Redwood-slat fences darkened to crimson-brown under fading daylight.

Some of Amy's earliest memories were set at the cottage, and she believed herself intimate with its environment. But she had never viewed this perspective. She had always looked toward water, not from it. Disorientation was unfamiliar, the difference unnerving.

Victoria Maxwell broke the silence. "Can you spot your place?"

"I don't know yet," Amy said, scanning the horizon. "I think that's Crescent Beach, because there's the peninsula. But I need to find a landmark."

Tony was relieved by the exchange, brief as it was. At least they were talking.

Ice's crust had turned soupy. To the right, weathered tips of boulders peeked from the frozen field. Air felt warmer as they moved closer to shore, but Tony suspected that was an illusion.

"Let's not worry too much about walking right up to your property," he suggested. "In fifteen minutes we'll be on land. I hope there's some food at the cottage, because I'm starving."

"You're hungry?" Amy asked, reaching into her vest pocket. "I have two granola bars." She thrust a plastic sleeve toward him and offered another to Victoria.

"No thanks," Victoria said. "Listen, we should have a target to aim for, or else we could be walking an extra mile up the road. Four hours on ice isn't long enough for you?"

Halting while Amy calculated, Tony tore open the shiny wrapper.

"I know all the houses from the beach, but they look different from here." Amy pointed. "I think that's the footpath from shore. So Kam Road is to the left, behind that row of homes. We should angle this way more."

They changed trajectory. Tony's crunching drowned out gurgling noises in his stomach. Amy opened the other packet and removed one of the granola bars. She folded the wrapper around the other.

"That… over there." Victoria pointed toward a murky inkspot the size of a painter's tarp. A stagnant puddle was ladled onto the frozen terrain. "Is that water or a mirage?"

"I don't know," Tony said, squinting and lowering sunglasses from his nose.

"Could there be a hole in the ice?"

"This close to shore?" Tony said. "This is where ice is thickest. It's probably a dip in the surface that the sun has melted. A shallow puddle of standing water. Either way, let's steer clear. We'll skirt around it, just to be safe."

The girls continued walking. Tony drifted from Victoria's side until he lagged behind. Eating had energized him. Reaching down, he scooped a palmful of snowy mush from the surface. Soggy, more water than snow, he tried to pack it into a fist-sized orb. The result more closely resembled a golf ball, but it would do.

Someone needs to cut this tension, he thought. It's going to be a long night unless we all start to smile.

"Snowball fight!" he shouted, tossing the puny projectile high into the air, where it landed between them with a muted thud. "Me against the girls!"

Curious, a sly look spread across Amy's face. Victoria was not amused.

"No way!" Amy countered. "No boys against girls. Me against the lovebirds!" She kicked a puddle and its splashes dotted Victoria's jeans.

"Hey!" Victoria giggled, leaping back. "You're lucky we're ten minutes from a warm house. If you're going to drench me, I want to take on both of you!"

"Okay, every man for himself!" Tony yelled.

"Every woman for herself," Amy corrected, pressing a withered snowball of her own, lobbing it in Tony's direction. Victoria saw this and began charging toward him. Amy snickered as Tony stagger-stepped, cutting left, anticipating Victoria's approach like he was trying to juke a defensive back. He laughed, planning to wrap his arms around her waist, when the floor of ice collapsed beneath him and he dropped into frigid water.

The girls began screaming before he surfaced.

* * *

Saturday, February 19, 1994 | 4:18 p.m.

Tony's jeans grew heavy with wetness. They added another thousand pounds to his body, and flutter kicking fatigued his legs. Pants are so damn cold they're not doing me any good, he thought. Just weighing me down. Reaching to his waist, struggling to peer through refraction, he fumbled, attempting to unbuckle the belt. Panting, nostrils plunked through the water's surface as he looked down. The sensation of having his face underwater frightened him further. Head snapping back, he made a decision to steady his eyes upward. Working solely by instinct — fingers were too desensitized to feel — he squiggled the buckle loose, groping for the zipper and its top button. An all-over chill gripped his body. Icy numbness burned skin like an orange flame.

Amy and Victoria yelled, their shrieked high-pitched words tumbling faster than Tony could process. His core temperature plunged. Comprehension dulled; thoughts grew muddy. He felt dizzy, dreamlike, treading against a thin soupy pool. His mind wandered drunkenly. He forced himself to concentrate on the jeans.

Although nerve endings had numbed his hands, Tony succeeded in loosening the button and zipper. Like a snake shedding its outer skin, he wriggled legs and pushed palms against hips. The soggy jeans peeled from his body slowly, bunching at the boots. Shackled by denim cuffs, he tucked legs toward his chin, keeping his mouth and nose above the water line. Tony gave two decisive yanks and the Levi's fell away, leaving his legs bare, exposed to icy water.

This was the wrong impulse to follow. Tony's pants were wet, but they added valuable insulation, and rapid loss of body heat brought him nearer to death. When his body temperature fell below eighty-five degrees, irrationality took over. Understanding of the situation slipped away.

Waving a green jacket like a blurred raceway flag, Amy was shouting to him from above, but sounds slurred. He had to focus now, he knew, but Amy's voice was a gaggle of migrating geese. Clear the head, concentrate, think…

* * *

Amy Black watched helplessly. Twenty feet away, Victoria's

body flailed on all fours as if gripped by seizure. In the time it took to blink, ice cracked and she exploded down into the turbid water, swallowed whole. Victoria's shrieking screams of doom gave way to silence. In the long beat of time when noise ceased, Amy was paralyzed, cloaked in disbelief.

Then she projected a desperate, high-pitched wail, like a wounded animal ensnared by an iron trap.

Abandoned on the frozen laketop, Amy was the only one left. Panic stabbed her gut, but she was still standing, not battling cold water or disorientation. She needed to employ logic and think for Tony and Victoria. Her mind raced: how could she pull her friends from the lake without falling in herself?

She had no rope, nothing to use as an anchor point. Surrounding ice was fragile, so she could not venture too close to existing holes. Odds were against her, but she must not go under herself. If she fell in, salvation was lost.

* * *

When weakened ice shattered beneath Victoria Maxwell, being submerged compounded her terror. Her mouth and nose suddenly filled with water, swallowing fearful screams. Her throat burned and she coughed reflexively, but still the chill slithered into her stomach. She tried to spit, yet her head had not yet broken the surface. She could not exhale without gulping more water.

Shocked to find herself in a maelstrom, Victoria lost a sense of direction. Kicking wildly, she was oblivious to the path of rising air bubbles. Flailing arms and legs pushed her ahead fifteen feet, under cover of a solid ice sheet. She searched for the opening she had fallen through, but disorientation was her enemy. The frigid lake was murky; coldness stung her pupils when she tried to peer underwater. Without air in her lungs, choking triggered panic. She could not pause to think while arctic water rushed into her throat. Light was dim, diluted, like illumination through a stained glass window. Clenching her eyes closed, she fluttered toward its faintness.

Victoria's head clunked against the bottom edge of ice. Its dull, colorless sheet was flat and hard, solid as corrugated steel. There was no air pocket in which she could breathe. Opening her mouth to scream again, her stomach drew in more water. She raised her hands and pushed against the pane, weakly pounding its mute surface.

Oxygen was being cut off from her brain. Blurred consciousness swam before her. A kaleidoscope of psychedelic lights glittered and danced behind closed pupils. She thought, scissor kick, find air, rest...

Within minutes of falling into Lake Erie, Victoria Maxwell's body, in spite of its natural protective reactions, suffered asphyxiation. Her heart stopped beating.

* * *

Amy Black had removed her down vest and stepped forward tentatively. Tony's head bobbed in the gentle chop, cheeks drained to the color of paste. He shivered forcefully, teeth chattering. His body spasmed.

"Victoria," he called out, but his voice was feeble, like a stage whisper. Amy could not be sure if he was addressing her, standing above, or his girlfriend, who would be unable to hear. "Did she go under?"

"Stay calm," Amy implored. "I'll get as close as I can and

use this jacket to pull you out."

She crept forward, extending the vest, nervous that ice might shatter beneath her. Five yards away, she lowered herself onto all fours and stretched prone, reasoning there was less risk of ice collapse if she spread her weight across a larger area. Tony's eyes were wild now, frenzied and confused. "I've got to get her," he vowed, inhaling deeply.

"No!" Amy shouted. "Tony, wait! If we get you out first, it'll be easier to save her!"

Tony heard the words but did not process them. Lungs filled with air, cheeks inflated comically like a puffer fish, Tony plunged underwater. Bare legs kicking as he descended into the miasma, his skittering mind believed he was capable of heroics.

* * *

Amy Black stood alone on the windswept plain, sweater and jeans absorbing sunrays. Her twisted stomach clenched as if filled with lead ingots. Below, current churned. Through open cracks, bubbles pushed ahead, their motion a cruel, haunting taunt. Her friends had been submerged long enough that they would not surface again.

Amy was alone.

Tony and Victoria were dead.

In a shoulder-shaking lament, Amy screamed at the sky. "Why? Why?" She choked on tears.

Her father was dead. Her roommate. Her closest friend, the man with whom she believed — only hours ago, before this hike began — she might have had a future.

Find the goodness in this day, she thought. See if there is a silver lining to this.

"Why, Lord?" she asked aloud. "What should I do? Give me a sign!"

Silence became deafening now, an elephant's trumpet that blurred her vision. She had nothing left. Nothing. Within eleven months, three of the people Amy cared most about had died, each one instantly, without reason. In compunction, she implored again.

"Why? Why are people I love snatched away?" she wailed. "Tell me what to do!"

The absence of sound was so pure that Amy Black wondered if shock had induced temporary deafness. She clapped her palms, listening for an echo. Scouring the Canadian shore for a sign of life, she detected no movement, no help. She pivoted toward Buffalo, but it was too distant to offer solace. Buildings could be seen, but not people. Cars atop the elevated bridge there were colored dots chugging forward without sound.

The safe choice would be to backtrack. It would take a few hours, and darkness would soon fall, but she could follow the lights and return to the American shore. The prospect of hiking during nighttime terrified her. Canada was close, close enough to hear her shout, but the risk of collapsing ice was too great to proceed.

Amy raised her eyes heavenward. Sky was a clear powder blue, its horizon empty of clouds. No interruption of color, no swirling gulls against pastel. Empty, barren nothingness.

She was completely alone.

No sign anywhere.

And Amy realized that was the sign. The absence of everything represented her life, where loved ones and dreams and hopes and logic and order were sucked downward into a giant, invisible vacuum, a beastly belly ingesting everything she had ever valued. There was no future for her, nothing to care about, no reason to anticipate another day.

Knees collapsed in surrender. Dead weight crumbled to the frozen plain, shoulders heaving. Tears poured freely until their reservoir had emptied. Ducts became a dried well, a seasonal drought devoid of moisture, yet still she shook uncontrollably.

Huddled in a fetal position, raised knees and crossed arms shrunk her into a collapsing ball of hurt. Pity descended upon the scene — a tattered crimson blanket of shame covering a broken figure, abandoned and alone.

20

Since becoming a widow, Lena Malone found solace in two things: photography and her dogs. The first was an interest she developed thirty years ago, the second borne of necessity. If not for the neighborhood robberies several winters before, she would never have adopted a pair of Great Danes. Now she was startled to consider what life had been like without them.

Straining against their collars, pulling leashes taut from her shrunken hand, Sir Ector and Sir Kay sniffed fresh humid air and spotted the path descending to the dormant beach. They yelped and yanked in unison. Lena balanced a camera strap across one shoulder, angling her waif-like body backwards to halt their straining progress. The lads loved the freedom of running unabated on snowdrifts and frozen sand, but Lena was not ready to set them free yet.

Crescent Beach's neighborhood was deserted, as it was every winter, in spite of today's warmth. Lena had thought that perhaps mild temperatures would bring seasonal residents back to their shuttered cottages for a mid-winter inspection.

Owners could see if ice had damaged the clapboard exteriors, or if plywood boards had loosened from snug window fittings. Although these homes clung to the lake's lee shore, protected on the west by a gentle curve of land extending into water, nature's spectral onslaught of snow and ice had a way of reaching around, between and over evergreens and concrete retaining walls. There was no evidence that anyone had come to check — in fact, the area was eerily quiet.

Air smelled like spring, hinting of pine cones and coming warmth — an unusual scent for February. It's too early, Lena thought. Yesterday and today were nice, but we're going to be paying for this deep into April, possibly even May. It's going to be a late thaw this year.

On the pebble-ridden concrete sidewalks, melting snow flooded into narrow rivulets. Shallow puddles filled earthy indentations. Beneath towering pines, matted needles, hardened from winter, lined the road. The Danes pitched ahead with enthusiasm. Lena considered releasing them. But if there were kids on the beach, unseen from here, perhaps around the breakwall or the grand summer cottage to the left, it could be dangerous. She tightened her grip on the leather straps, whispering soothing words.

"Easy boys," she cooed. "We'll be there soon enough. If there's no one around you can run like demons while I take photos."

Lena's voice was marked by a distinctive Canadian accent in which vowels were polished smooth. She had been raised in Hamilton, an hour north of Crescent Beach, and lived there with her husband until his passing four years earlier. Thanks to a generous insurance policy, Lena was financially secure. Now, gray-haired in her early fifties, she believed herself too young to be paralyzed by widowhood and too old to find another mate. Her children moved away, one lured by a job in Vancouver, the other attending university in Ottawa. With no desire to remain in the empty split-level, she did something her kids could not have predicted: she sold the home and bought a two-bedroom bungalow only blocks from Crescent Beach, committed to living here year-round.

She had loved the neighborhood for thirty years, having visited friends at their cottage so long ago. There were amenities nearby — grocery stores and restaurants — but it was secluded enough to satisfy her love of nature: old growth maple and oak trees, proximity to Lake Erie, and hiking trails converted from former rail lines. The area was ripe for her photographer's vision. Living within walking distance of a Great Lake meant she would always have a subject to shoot.

The only drawback was that her children were too far away. But at least she would spend the next week with her older son — she was boarding a flight to Vancouver the following day. Perhaps, she thought, I can capture some poetic pictures of Lake Erie to share with him.

The camera, insulated by a canvas carry sack, was familiar against her shoulder. Lugging equipment, cumbersome as it might be, was part of the tradeoff. A warm day like this could reap dividends. Crusty layers of the lake's top would melt, bubbling into interesting cracks and puddles. Snap a few exposures, capture sunlight glinting against the brightened tint. Framed the proper way, she might get lucky and create something riveting.

Snowdrifts had dissolved into uneven patches along the curve of the beach. Sand, loose and grainy during warm months, was packed hard, as if lacquered with epoxy. The ground did not crunch when Lena or the Danes stepped there — in fact, there was no audible or visible displacement. Although air was warm, heat had yet to absorb into earth. The loam remained gripped by winter freeze.

Just offshore, water-smoothed boulders poked through ice. The area was legendary for its rocky shallows and uneven depths. Although schools of small mouth bass clustered around these boulders in summer, most fishermen avoided maneuvering boats too close for fear of splitting a hull. Since Lena's arrival, two snowmobilers drowned here when ice collapsed beneath the weight of their machines.

Reaching the trail's end, rounding the corner, Lena scanned the beach. Deserted. As if begging permission for their impending freedom, the Danes whimpered meekly.

"All right, boys," she muttered, unclipping the leashes. "This is your last run here until I get back from Vancouver, so enjoy. Next time we do this, it's going to be cold again."

With only a moment's delay, Sir Ector and Sir Kay bounded along the shore, long legs settling into a loping rhythm. Lena watched them go, smiling, then removed the camera bag from her shoulder. Squatting to unpack the Nikon, she spooled a new roll of black and white film into the camera's back.

Sun was beginning its evening descent, and Lena knew that shadows created by fading winter light provided interesting contrasts. She had been taught to compose photos using the rule of three — divide the picture in thirds both by length and height, so it resembled a tic-tac-toe board with nine invisible squares. Action points should be slightly askew, intersecting any of the four corners edging the middle box. Off-center symmetry was an optical invitation to become part of the picture. Amateur photographers made the frequent mistake of framing everything in the middle, which was boring, uninteresting.

Lena looped the strap around her neck and attached the long, cylindrical lens. Raising the camera to her nose, squinting one eye closed, she surveyed the scene through the viewfinder. Its telephoto capacity diminished distances. Through contoured glass, she was suddenly nearer to textured ice. Buffalo's skyline was hidden around a grove of trees, but the horizon just south of downtown felt close enough to touch.

Lena snapped a few shots of the deserted steel mill there, attentive to angling shadows. She turned her attention to pockets of open water and the gurgling current that cut from underneath. Swinging the lens to the right, Lena exhaled in surprise as three figures sprang into her vision.

She lowered the camera and gazed in that direction. Sure enough, there were people on the frozen surface! Were they skating? Cross country skiing? What the heck would they be doing out there on a warm day like this?

Before those thoughts took root, Lena snapped a half dozen photos, hoping to capture the oddity of it all. Clusters of three were visually stimulating, better than a pair. Unevenness and lack of symmetry lured the eye. Complimented with the unique setting, this had potential for an artsy picture, one she could show to her son.

She could not see much of the three, even through the telephoto. Two women and a man. But there was no way to gauge their ages, or know what they were doing on the lake. It appeared they were moving towards Canada, although Lena considered the direction could be an optical illusion.

Within ten minutes, the roll was spent. Lena called the dogs back. They trotted lazily, tongues panting, allowing her to refasten leashes against their collars. The camera tucked safely in its blue bag, slung over her shoulder, Lena led the

Danes up the path, away from the beach, toward home.

She was out of sight and earshot when Amy Black began to scream.

* * *

Later that evening, in the comfort of her darkroom, Lena Malone examined the flimsy strip of black and white negatives. She thought two frames had potential, so she fitted them into the enlarger. Projected onto a flat formica table, her eye hesitated. She found nothing interesting about the composition or subject matter. Even with the telephoto lens, figures were too far away to appear distinct. She could detect few details: the two women wore knit caps, while the man's hair blew free in the wind. Otherwise, facial features were miniscule, washed out, erased by distance and shadow. The negatives were pedestrian — there was nothing to justify making prints.

Lena twisted the film into a loose spool and threw it into the garbage can by the darkroom door, one of thousands of rolls that simply did not make the cut.

She hauled a plastic garbage bag to the curb the following morning, dropped the Danes at a kennel, and flew to Vancouver to spend a week with her son. Lena Malone never learned that three people died on Lake Erie, or that her pictures were the last living record of Tony Davenport, Amy Black and Victoria Maxwell.

21

Middle of the night calls, admittedly rare, were part of the job that Captain David McClusky despised. In that gasping moment between sleep and recognition of a ringing phone, his mind pattered with questions. Molly? Her sleeping form was curled beside him, warm and dark. Thoughts were muddy as he struggled for comprehension. Megan? Had she been home last night? Peter? Might he have snuck out, as teenage boys sometimes did, to muster trouble? Or were the kids down the hall, as expected, safely asleep in their rooms?

Pulled from deep tranquility, his dry throat clenched with alarm. Leaning across the nightstand, he fumbled in darkness for the receiver.

"McClusky," he said, without moving lips.

"David, you've got to get in here," the dispatcher's raspy voice ordered. "At first light we need you up in Sky One to look for some missing kids."

"Kids?" he echoed. "Megan? Peter?"

"Megan? Peter? Hell, are you awake?" the scratchy voice asked abruptly, oblivious to McClusky's sleep patterns. "Not your kids. Three different kids. In their twenties. A friend of theirs is saying they went out on the lake for a hike, and no one can locate any of them."

"What time is it?"

"It's early," the dispatcher admitted. "Four-thirtyish. But get in here right away. When light breaks the horizon, we want your eyes up there. Nobody's heard from them since Saturday."

"Saturday?" McClusky rubbed his nose. "What's today? Monday? They can't still be out there."

"We don't know where they are. Their trajectory was to leave from Hamburg and cross to Crescent Beach. One of the kids lived in a cottage there. But no one can find them on either shore."

"Crescent Beach? That's dangerous. Strange water patterns."

"Yeah, at this point we don't know what we're dealing with." The pause suggested gravity in the dispatcher's words. "If this shakes out like I think, we're probably looking at recovery, not rescue."

* * *

Being of Irish heritage in South Buffalo during the 1950s meant that the Roman Catholic catechism governed your life. You did not eat meat on Fridays, only fish; you attended mass every Sunday and the first Friday of each month; you knew rosary prayers and were devout during holy days of obligation; you did not consume anything except water before receiving the communion host on Sunday mornings. Easter was the most important annual holiday, because that was when Christ rose from the dead so that sin could be forgiven, although children selfishly preferred Christmas because they received presents. With more than 710,000 Catholics in Western New York in 1955, religion was the centerpiece of life, and the McClusky family adhered to its tenets.

David's father worked at Bethlehem Steel while his mother stayed home to raise kids. The 1950s were simpler days — the word "homemaker" had not yet come into vogue, nor had the hyphenated phrase "Irish-American." His mom cooked meals, washed laundry, supervised children. The family proudly called itself Irish, harboring muted suspicion of other ethnicities. Instead of street names as borders, neighborhoods were defined by the parish its Catholics attended. The McCluskys were parishioners at Holy Family, while a few blocks away, residents claimed loyalty to Our Lady of Victory. Beyond that, St. Theresa's, St. Thomas Aquinas or St. Ambrose.

Catholicism's inherent values anchored David McClusky's family, rooting early and sprouting as years passed. His older brother, Patrick, entered the seminary and became a priest. More than once, David listened to his brother boast from the pulpit — only half-jokingly — how anyone who had lived in South Buffalo knew, in spite of Israelites' claims, that this was truly the promised land.

In large part, faith and Catholic values drew David Mc-Clusky into law-enforcement. Raised with the structure of rules and order, he believed in moral imperatives, understanding a responsibility to those in need. He sought to spread good works to a wider domain than parish boundaries.

McClusky's faith was often evident when he flew Sky One over Lake Erie. He recalled opening words from Genesis: "In the beginning, when God created the heavens and the earth, the earth was a formless wasteland, and darkness covered the abyss, while a mighty wind swept over the waters." McClusky considered that scripture passage could be written from this vantage point, in the cockpit of a helicopter overlooking the Great Lake.

Weather and time of year dictated the view below. Most winters, the lake froze, crusting into a cover of white. During freezing or melting, white swirled with blue, like God poured food coloring onto His palette. McClusky had tried to describe the sight to Molly, but labored for words, finding vocabulary inadequate. He wondered if better storytellers than he could give justice to such magnificence.

The starkness brought McClusky closest to his Catholicism. This was the planet on the second day, when God had created only water, light and sky. How many people will ever witness this sight? he wondered. Could seeing this alter one's perception and create a path to spirituality? When planes cross overhead, do passengers stare down from their tiny portholes to appreciate this? Do they reevaluate their pithy, everyday problems? Do they reflect on man's insignificance, their smallness relative to the raw power of God? Can such humility transform one's life?

Now, as the number of Catholics dwindled — the early 1990s reported thirty years of steady losses — parishes closed and congregations merged. Patrick recalled the peak years of the 1970s, when there were more than 1,000 priests, 2,500 nuns, 300 parishes and a Catholic population approaching one million.

"I've got a foolproof way to get your numbers back up," David McClusky joked with his brother. "In fact, I could convert atheists to Christianity. All I need to do is get them up in the helicopter during winter and show them Lake Erie."

* * *

The previous winter, McClusky accompanied Molly to her office Christmas party. Uncomfortable around strangers, he tried to be unobtrusive near the hors d'ouvres table, squirming in a tie, while Molly did her usual social butterfly act, working the room with gaiety. A chunky middle-aged woman in a blue blazer approached him and began talking. She introduced herself, but McClusky did not retain her name. She was unsteady on her feet.

"So what do you do?" she wondered.

"I work for the Sheriff's Department," he said.

Recognition flashed in her eyes as she aimed a finger at him. "You're the helicopter pilot. You do rescues, right? I've heard Molly talk about it."

"Right."

"Let me ask you something," the woman droned, leaning too close. McClusky could smell alcohol as she exhaled. "Why a helicopter?"

"What do you mean?"

"Why not a plane? Do you use a helicopter because it's got the word hell in it?" The woman cackled at her own joke. "I mean, is there really a difference?"

McClusky explained the advantages of movement a helicopter affords. A plane can travel three basic directions: forward, up and down. But a helicopter was three-dimensional. In addition to forward, up and down, one could move backwards, or stop and hover, depending on adjustments the pilot made.

"It allows much more flexibility for rescues, especially in a tight situation, like a gorge." McClusky said. "If I hover and rotate, I can get a 360-degree view."

Shortly the woman's husband materialized, shaking hands with McClusky as she introduced him. He was a squat, balding fellow who worked as an engineer. Unlike his wife, he was sober and serious.

"If you understand the way a helicopter operates, you'll never get into one again," the man volunteered. He proceeded to explain how the cyclic controls lateral direction while the collective was responsible for up and down motion. Foot pedals adjusted the tail rotor to keep the helicopter pointed forward, and these could be manipulated to pivot in either direction on an axis.

McClusky knew all this. As a pilot, he was annoyed to receive a lecture from someone who admitted to having never flown. Was this dull man trying to impress his boozed-up wife? He was probably regurgitating a blurb from Popular Mechanics.

"There are a lot of things that could go wrong," the engineer warned. "Flying a helicopter is like balancing a broomstick on your fingertip. It can be done, but you'd better play complete attention and hope for a little luck. One mistake and you stall. You stall up there and it's goodbye California." McClusky did not understand how California entered the equation, but quickly tired of the man's dire warnings.

"Too many moving parts," the man chided. "Engineers don't like moving parts."

"There's a joke there somewhere," the woman chortled to McClusky, stabbing him with an elbow. "Fill in your own punch line."

"All I'm saying is you need to be careful," the man said, impatient with his wife.

"Be careful," McClusky repeated dryly. "I'll be sure to keep that in mind next time I lift off."

22

Television newscast
WGRZ-Channel 2-Buffalo

"After a weekend of balmy temperatures, it's back to reality for Western New York. Happy Monday morning, everyone. We'll get to our commuter's traffic report in a moment, but the big story here is the weather warmup this weekend. Kevin is standing by to give us an update."

"Thanks, Maryalice. I hope everyone enjoyed the warmth over the past few days, because it could be awhile before we see the mercury climb that high again. Let's look at the map with current temperatures and you can see things are becoming a bit more seasonal.

"Now going into the weekend, we knew Saturday would be mild, but Sunday was a real bonus. We can credit a mass of warm air that traveled all the way up from the Gulf of Mexico and lingered over the Great Lakes longer than expected. Late last night, however, reality returned. Winds began to pick up, shifting that warm air to the east, and temperatures started falling. In fact, as Sunday changed to Monday, the midnight reading was forty-one degrees. That, unfortunately, is going to be the high for today. Already, we're down below the freezing mark… and the bad news is that winds will increase and the temperature will continue to fall. This will make for some uncomfortable wind chills today.

"So I hope you kept the coat and mittens handy. It was a nice respite, but winter is back."

* * *

Monday, February 21, 1994 | 7:11 a.m.

Captain David McClusky had grown accustomed to loudness. Sky One's engine and whirling blades created a brain-pounding din, but his headset swallowed some of those decibels as he ran through a series of checks before takeoff. After twenty-five years, there were still elements of this job that impressed him. One was lifting off. As the helicopter sprung vertically into air, he felt superhuman. He marveled as the helipad fell away, like a tissue dropped into a darkened well. There was no secret how the helicopter leaped upward — it was a convergence of physics that could be explained scientifically. But on an emotional level, it was also a test of faith, one that belied conventional beliefs. Seemingly by miracle, he ascended above earth, chopper blades flapping rhythmically in a frenzied heartbeat. After clearing the treeline, the helicopter's nose dipped as it bounded ahead.

Stationed three miles inland in Hamburg, Sky One jaunted above neighborhoods before Lake Erie appeared in half light like a wrinkled muslin blanket. Dawn had begun to brighten the east. Below, vehicles' headlights were moving specks along Route 5. Long shadows fell into water.

"Ten minutes until we get some light," McClusky's words crackled into the headset. His partner, Danny Vargas, nodded. "For now let's make a pass to Crescent Beach. Maybe we'll get lucky."

Sky One maintained a 1,200-foot altitude. Height provided a geographic panorama — another job component that left McClusky awestruck. As daylight grew, Lake Ontario became visible to the north. The Niagara River bisected Buffalo from Canada. Bridges below were clear landmarks: the Peace Bridge's erector set truss; north of it, the abandoned Railroad Bridge, a series of connected trapezoids crouching low to the waterline. Twin spans on the north and south ends of Grand Island arched east of the river's fork. In Buffalo, art deco City Hall stretched in front of other downtown high rises. Limiting waterfront access, a highway sprouted cloverleaf exit ramps.

But Erie was their focus. At this hour, the lake was a faded Technicolor moonscape. There was a dreamlike quality to its field, an abstract expression of dulled blues and opaque swirling into marble expanse like a vast, primordial swath of cold. Hues blended so subtly that, in growing light, it was not possible to tell where the snow-ice mixture ended and water encroached its edges.

Flying at eighty miles per hour, they spanned the international boundary in minutes. As Canada's shore grew visible, Vargas pointed.

"There are all kinds of holes in that ice, Cap," he said. "Wind is going to keep those cracks moving around a bit."

"Dammit," McClusky muttered, rolling the helicopter left.

"This is not what we want."

"Open spots have probably been shifting for the past two days," Vargas said. "This could be a needle in a haystack."

Neither officer spotted anything to indicate missing people, but McClusky remained undaunted. He dipped lower, scanning the vista. Dawn's newness inspired hope. McClusky decreased the helicopter's speed almost to a hover, slowly crisscrossing ice in a loose grid pattern. They began combing the American shore, moving in a curved line from the city southward toward Hamburg. When that pass turned up nothing, they doubled back, sliding farther onto the lake, away from land.

"Dispatcher said this was probably going to be recovery, not rescue," Vargas reminded his partner.

"Let's concentrate on the Canadian side. Fort Erie is treacherous. Remember the snowmobilers a couple years ago?"

Vargas nodded. "What do we know about the victims?"

"I talked to the friend who reported them missing," Mc-Clusky answered. "Polish kid named Jablonski. He was pretty much a wreck. He didn't tell me much the dispatcher hadn't gotten already, but I asked about their families."

"Yeah?"

"The two girls share an apartment in Buffalo. One has been staying at a cottage off Crescent Beach. Dad's dead, and mom lives in Amherst. She's being contacted right now. The other girl is from Ohio, so I'm letting Smitty track that down. The guy grew up in Hamburg. Moved to the city when his parents retired to Florida."

Vargas shook his head. "Grew up in Hamburg and didn't know enough to stay off the lake when it's sixty-three degrees?"

From the southern shore of Fort Erie, ice was dotted with openings like ragged potholes. McClusky lowered the helicopter close enough that protruding rocks were visible from the cockpit. Sky One swept along the coast westward toward Point Abino. Telltale signs of winter were apparent: boats and pilings drydocked on higher ground, beaches desolate. There were no people — nor signs anyone might have traversed this route.

But on the return pass, a half mile from land, a colored lump on the helicopter's right flank caught McClusky's eye. He slowed immediately and altered direction, angling his head.

"There," he said to Vargas. "What is that?"

Vargas lifted binoculars to his face while McClusky slowed to hover. Below, on a flat plain of ice, was a discarded ball of fabric. It was the only color amid a peppering of open holes.

"Crumpled overcoat, I think," Vargas pronounced. "Tough to tell. Go lower. Would you agree it's green?"

"Yeah, that's how I saw it." McClusky swallowed. "Radio in and have Smitty find out if any of them wore a green jacket."

* * *

Within two hours, as wind increased, the surrounding area had been sprayed with colored dye to mark its location against shifting ice fields. The U.S. Coast Guard dispatched a cutter to Crescent Beach, but its travel was slow, chopping through ragged ice and nefarious water.

The lake was scanned with an infrared device to detect irregular shapes. Technology showed a minefield of sunken boulders, but nothing resembling human form was found. A

Coast Guard team plunged an underwater camera into the abyss, but images it reflected were dark and murky, and after a few hours, searchers were no closer to finding bodies.

In fact, there was no sign of three missing people anywhere near the recovered vest.

23

Buffalo News: Tuesday, February 22, 1994. Front page.

3 FRIENDS MISSING ON LAKE ERIE ICE
Searchers fear victims drowned during hike

A search for three missing Buffalo residents continued today as crews attempted to drag the waters of Lake Erie for bodies of presumed drowning victims. Shifting ice fields and high winds made the job more difficult.

The man and two women apparently disappeared under ice while hiking between Hamburg and Crescent Beach, Ont., on Saturday.

Monday night, the victims were identified as Anthony Davenport, 25, and Victoria Maxwell, 26, both of Buffalo. Also missing is Amy Black, 28, who shares a Buffalo apartment with Ms. Maxwell.

A friend told police Monday that the three had planned to travel across the lake on Saturday. The abandoned vehicles of Davenport and Maxwell were found parked at Hamburg

Beach. Ms. Maxwell's wallet was discovered in the glove compartment of her car.

Search crews later spotted a partially submerged vest in a field of ice about a half mile from the Canadian shore. According to Hamburg police, the jacket was identified as belonging to Ms. Black.

Plans were underway to launch an Erie County Sheriff's Department boat today equipped with a grappling hook, but shifting ice fields left a larger hole of open water than existed during the weekend. The changing ice patterns make it difficult to pinpoint where the bodies entered the water.

"Inclement weather is going to decrease the probability of locating them," said Capt. David McClusky, commander of the Erie County Sheriff Department's search and rescue team.

Helicopters piloted by the Erie County Sheriff's Department and the U.S. Coast Guard patrolled the area Monday, crisscrossing during a late-morning search. The Coast Guard used an infrared scanning device, and one area was marked with green dye. By late afternoon, high winds halted further operations.

Capt. McClusky said the water off Crescent Beach has varying depths, generally between 15 and 20 feet. He planned to return to the site with deputies and resume the search as soon as conditions are safe to fly.

"There is a current there, but that won't have much affect on the bodies," he said. "They would sink right to the bottom."

Authorities based the assumption about three friends' drownings on the fact that none of them could be located Monday morning. A friend's report of their planned hike and the abandoned vehicles support this theory.

Ms. Black was expected at South Park High School, where she has been an art teacher for the past three years.

"She's an enthusiastic teacher who gets good results from the kids," said John Keefe, the school's principal. "As far-fetched as it sounds, we're holding out hope that this is some misunderstanding and she'll turn up alive."

Details on the other two victims were sketchy as of Monday, but authorities said Ms. Black and Ms. Maxwell shared an apartment on Richmond Avenue.

"I don't know much about them," said a neighbor, who asked to not be identified. "They seemed pretty quiet to me."

* * *

Tuesday, February 22, 1994 | 10:37 a.m.

Jill Barto was angry. She read the newspaper, unlike many of her stupid classmates. She learned the facts surrounding Miss Black's disappearance. None of the other students made an effort. All they did was pass along rumors and innuendo, most of which were ludicrous.

"I heard Miss Black was cross-country skiing on the ice with a concussion and got lost," one girl boldly proclaimed before art class.

"I heard she had legal trouble so she had to live in Canada," another added.

Such gossip made Jill Barto froth with rage. It was bad enough that some wrinkled old pruny hobbit had stepped into Miss Black's class as a substitute teacher. He didn't know the first thing about art. His was just a warm body to ensure that kids didn't riot or run amok. And what was with this principal, Mr. Keefe, who was mute about the incident? Shouldn't he come on the loudspeaker and make an announcement or something? Sure, he sang Miss Black's praises in the paper, but how about saying something to the kids she actually taught? We're the people she cared about, not strangers who read the news. Wouldn't that be proper decorum?

Yesterday morning Jill had reported to the classroom, as Miss Black directed her, anxious to see her teacher's portfolio. She was upbeat, Monday morning notwithstanding. Jill would get a glimpse into the life of a real artist, and Miss Black was so nice. But the door was locked, and through the frosted glass panel lights were off, so no one was inside. Laying books on her lap, Jill sat on the hallway floor, leaning against the wall. Miss Black must be running late.

When homeroom bell rang and her teacher had yet to appear, Jill became annoyed. Now she would be tardy and face detention. Should she wait another few minutes and get a pass when Miss Black finally arrived? After all, it was her fault Jill was late.

A day later, anger from being forgotten had morphed to guilt. Jill pouted most of Monday, only to learn this morning that Miss Black disappeared and a full-scale search was underway. Had she been alive on the ice yesterday morning while I waited impatiently outside her classroom? If I had reported to the main office that my teacher was absent, would they have contacted authorities? Would someone have been able to save her? Am I responsible because I didn't come clean right away?

Miss Black was the sole good thing about this miserable school, and now she was gone — likely for good.

"I'm sorry for Miss Black and everything," one of the preppy girls said in the cafeteria. "But that's not the brightest thing she could have done. I bet even Tex here knows enough not to walk across Lake Erie."

Jill Barto's anger exploded. She overturned the girl's plastic cafeteria tray, scattering pizza and fries across the table and into her lap. A puddle of milk dribbled to the floor. The cavernous room turned quiet. Hundreds of eyes burned into Jill, who held a challenging stance.

"Shut up!" Jill yelled, pointing a finger at the airheaded girl. "Just shut up about Miss Black!"

24

Compassion was one thing. If there was a no-fault accident, Janet Long could brim with empathy. That time a bus swerved on a wet highway and three kids were killed. The driver couldn't get straight with the guilt, although it was not his fault a deer leaped in front of the grille. He simply reacted like anyone would, wrenching the wheel, causing the overturn. Within a year, he drank himself stupid and jammed a gun in his mouth. Wrong place, wrong time, no blame. The situation deserved compassion.

Or when that city councilman's fifteen-year-old hijacked a Firebird and cracked up going the wrong way on the Thruway. The kid was a mope, but you had to feel for his dad, especially after his wife had fallen to cancer the previous summer.

See? She could be sympathetic in the proper context. Compassion for people behaving stupidly was another thing altogether.

Janet Long was not a nurturer, and the managing editor knew it. Still, he assigned her this story. She wondered why.

"It's got the makings of a real heart-wringer, Jan," the bald man said earlier in the day, wagging a finger before her. She hated when people shortened her name, and the little weasel knew it. "You gotta find the right voice for this, the right tone. These three kids are average folks — they're Buffalo people, you know? They eat pizza and wings on Friday night. We all know somebody like this. They're everybody's kid or neighbor. They made a grave error in judgment that led them to…"

Their grave? Janet thought.

"Well, that's bad word choice," the managing editor continued after a pause, "but you know what I'm saying, right? Readers need to identify with them. They have to be seen as real people, full round characters in the springtime of life."

Janet groaned internally.

"I got word their friends are meeting tonight at this bar on Main Street. Very informal, just a way to get together and remember their pals. I want you there to do a feature. Find out who these kids were. Talk to their friends. What made them tick?"

Lovely, Janet thought. Three kids don't know enough to stay off Lake Erie when it's sixty-three degrees, and there go my evening plans. I'll have to call my husband and tell him—

"You should highlight the senselessness of this tragedy," her boss droned, sliding a palm over his clean pate. "These kids didn't deserve to be victims. They didn't have to die. I want you to find the right tales, in a proper, mournful tenor. I want this feature to resonate with the average reader. You know, could this happen to me, that kind of vein. You do this right, we could be looking at front page."

Like any veteran journalist, Janet had an acquired ability to remain emotionally detached. Stay in this business long enough, and you'll pretty much see it all. But lead story or not, the assignment would take all the patience she could muster.

* * *

Tuesday, February 22, 1994 | 8:57 p.m.

In the dimly lit room, at the bar's far corner, a fortysomething man perched on a stool, tiny palms curved around a frosted glass of draft. His short hair was sandy, neutral fading to gray, cropped close enough on the sides that his scalp was visible in the neon glow. His eyes were bright blue marbles, small and crafty; the point of his nose flattened, as if sheared away. The man's movements were sharp and jerky, like a sparrow scouring a damp field for food.

"Look at those kids," he said to the bartender. His voice was high pitched, almost feminine. "Sitting around talking about those morons in reverent tones. I'm telling you Eddie, it's all I can do to go over there right now and slap some sense into them. I mean, what the hell were they thinking?"

"Go easy, Martin," the bartender said. Instead of dulling his senses, Martin became emboldened by alcohol. Highstrung, jittery, the compact man was devoted to current events. Last weekend, when Dan Jansen won a gold medal on his last attempt in Olympic speedskating, Martin wept with the spirituality of a religious convert. A few months earlier, after information about Nancy Kerrigan's bashed knee came to light, he tried to rally a lynching party and make a pilgrimage to the Northwest, where Tonya Harding lived, to extract revenge. The bartender had grown accustomed to Martin working himself into unnecessary frenzies.

"I mean, let's be honest. Did these kids know what they

were doing? You don't just walk across Lake Erie without serious planning and preparation. It's not a pond. It's got a fast current cutting through it. It's almost like a river."

"All right, Martin."

"I mean, did they take life jackets? Did they take a spud bar? How about rope, or flares, or spikes? Did they even declare they were leaving the country? This isn't like walking across the street. You're entering an entirely different nation when you go to Canada. You got to let customs in on your fun. Would you try walking across the German border into Poland without letting somebody know?"

"What's a spud bar?" the bartender asked. "It's a walking stick. Old-school fishermen would keep it in front of them and stab the ice to test it before every step. Those old-timers respected the lake. They knew you should be scared to go out there, and only go if you took precautions."

"It's a sad story," the bartender agreed, but Martin continued as if he had not heard.

"I've spent my life in that water. I've been on that lake in winter. I've actually been out there when the ice cracked. It's some scary shit. Sounds like a cannon! It's deafening, like God's clapping his hands. A split like that can span thirty miles. And then, if the surface of the crack refreezes, it would look just the same as thicker ice around it, but it would be too feeble to support a person's weight. You would have no idea you were stepping onto danger until you broke through into water.

"Another thing about that lake," Martin continued, stabbing the air with an index finger. "You can't tell how far away things are just by looking. It's full of optical illusions. I mean, you stand on Hamburg Beach, and Canada is just so damn inviting. But it looks a lot closer than it really is. It's like trying to measure a desert when you're in the middle of it. It's a straight view that becomes deceptive. There's no obstructions or landmarks to gauge, so the distance fools you. Those kids probably thought, hell, it's a half hour walk, we can be to Canada in no time."

Martin exhaled deeply, like a pressure cooker releasing accumulated buildup. "I'm telling you, Eddie, I'm tempted to plant myself in the middle of that group of kids and say something about how stupid their friends were. I really am."

Eddie knew that despite the tough talk, Martin would not do such a thing. Martin was, in fact, a coward — a barfly paralyzed by life who dealt with his insecurities by swallowing lager in a darkened neon glow. For all his bravado and inflated machismo, Martin was a timid, feeble being who clung to the shadows, content to spout his opinions where others were unwilling to respond.

"That woman over there," Eddie said, pointing to a booth across the room, "She's a newspaper reporter. Doing a story about the victims, trying to get background information."

Martin turned and studied the woman, huddled with a skinny kid over a rectangular table. "No shit? A reporter?" His mood turned introspective. He said, as if doing so would constitute a public service, "Maybe I'll go talk to her to set things straight."

* * *

Tuesday, February 22, 1994 | 8:57 p.m.

"This is the booth," Mark Jablonski pointed to the lacquered table before them, addressing the middle-aged newspaper reporter. He did not remember her name, although she had introduced herself before sitting down. Mark was awed by the length of her greying pony tail, which stretched almost to her tailbone, its style reminding him vaguely of the 1960s. "This is where Tony and I sat last time we came here. I ordered a bacon burger and he had a double order of medium wings. We split a pitcher of Labatt's Blue."

Janet Long kept her pad closed. Last fall she had stopped smoking and taken up yoga in a losing effort to delay effects of middle age. She had been faithful to her new healthy lifestyle. Now, sitting in a bar full of smoke and booze, she craved a cigarette to stifle irritability.

Patience would be imperative tonight. This skinny little runt was going to canonize his friends and talk about every little nuance of their years together. *This is the booth where we sat.* Who the hell cares? *He had a double order of medium wings.* How is that relevant to anything?

During the next few hours, tears would slither into people's drinks; three victims would be eulogized as if the pope was delivering orations from St. Peter's Square. Stories would be told, jokes shared, memories recollected. She had committed to getting the best story she could, even if this was not an assignment she would have chosen. That little flunky managing editor would turn cartwheels when he saw this article. But would her words sound judgmental? Could she write it without coming off smarmy?

"Look at all the people who came," Mark said, waving a hand toward the cluster before the bar, where some two dozen twentysomethings congregated. "I made exactly three calls today and said we should get together here, and it just snowballed. One guy called a couple more friends, and so on. It's a Tuesday night in the depths of winter, for God's sake. The number of people here is an indication of how well these three were liked."

"Tell me a little about Tony Davenport," Janet prompted, face betraying none of her brewing restlessness.

Mark gulped a swallow of beer, eyes hazing as he gazed beyond the room, looking into the past. "Tony… now there was a prince of a guy. My best friend since we took driver's ed together nine years ago. His heart was as big as his stomach, I used to tease. See, he played varsity football and used to be Mr. Fitness, but he kind of chunked out after high school. His generosity would fill this room. One time, at his apartment, we're standing in the kitchen talking, and he makes two peanut butter and jelly sandwiches. I wasn't even paying attention, I was so busy flapping my lip, but he cuts them both in half and slides one over to me on a paper towel. What's this? I ask. He goes, it's a sandwich, you moron. I say, I didn't ask for this. He says, well then give it back. I'll eat it. I'm hungry. I thought if you saw me eating one, you'd want one too."

The reporter opened her spiral pad and began scribbling abbreviated shorthand, filling its narrow pages. I'm not exactly going to lead with a peanut butter sandwich, she thought, but I've got to keep this snot-nose talking.

"You know why he wanted to be a teacher?" Mark continued. "Plain and simple, so he could help people. He used to say to me, real casual-like, Jabber, I think I can change a few lives. But even if I only help one kid in my career, then the world's a better place. I told him if he teaches for thirty years, he's bound to help more than just one kid. He said, Yup, that's the plan. I tell you, he was a prince of a guy…"

* * *

Buffalo News: Wednesday, February 23, 1994. Page B1, local section.

VICTIMS OF LAKE TREK RECALLED
AS PROMISING YOUNG PEOPLE
Earlier Harbor Stroll Led to Tragedy
By Janet Long

A short walk atop frozen ice in the Small Boat Harbor eleven days ago was the inspiration for three people to hike across Lake Erie last Saturday.

Anthony Davenport and Victoria Maxwell were awed by the winter scene, and hatched a plan for a longer hike from Hamburg Beach to Fort Erie with Amy Black, who lived in a cottage there.

The night before leaving, Davenport spoke to his friend Mark Jablonski.

"I wondered if what they were doing was safe," Jablonski said. "But Tony said he planned to call the Coast Guard to be sure."

On Tuesday, authorities continued to search for the missing bodies of Davenport, 25, Maxwell, 26, and Black, 28, before calling off operations in late afternoon. A U.S. Coast Guard icebreaker, using a grappling hook and underwater video camera, failed to locate them.

The Erie County Sheriff's Department has also suspended its search indefinitely due to changing weather patterns.

The three departed from Hamburg Beach on Saturday for the approximately ten-mile hike. They were apparently within a half mile of the Canadian shore, near Crescent Beach, before they broke through weakened ice and drowned.

In the wake of their deaths, people have questioned the wisdom of undertaking such a hike when temperature had climbed to 63 degrees. But Davenport reportedly called the Coast Guard late Friday or early Saturday to confirm conditions were safe.

"Ice is eighteen inches thick in some spots," said meteorologist Steve Chudzik of the National Weather Service. "Maybe they heard that and thought it was uniform depth for their entire route."

"It's sad, but Tony did what he wanted to do," said Jablonski, Davenport's close friend. "He had a sense of adventure that was infectious."

By all accounts, the three high-achievers were entering the prime of their lives.

Black was a third-year art teacher at South Park High School, where she founded an after-school art club and was involved in painting scenery for school musicals. On weekends, she tutored with Literacy Volunteers.

"She was a fine young teacher," said South Park principal John Keefe. "She was all about art, and the kids really responded to her. Everyone around here is pretty devastated about her loss."

As a Literacy Volunteers tutor, Black worked extensively with a young woman from El Salvador who was learning English as a second language. The experience was one she relished, according to friends.

"Amy helped her student fill out job applications, because that was something she struggled with," Jablonski said. "Within a week, the girl landed a factory job making good money. Amy told me how much respect she had for the young lady, coming to America to create a better life for herself. Amy called her a hero, but to me, Amy was the hero. Without her, the student never would have gotten a job. Amy was the springboard for success."

Black shared an apartment with Maxwell, but had been staying regularly at the family's Crescent Beach cottage.

Maxwell, a native of Toledo, Ohio, was a first year law student at the University at Buffalo, where she received an undergraduate degree in history in 1989 and played varsity volleyball before the program folded six years ago.

"She loved the law," said Garrett R. Burns, Admissions Director of UB's law school. "She was bright, energetic and perceptive. I know from our conversations that she planned to use the law to help people who were indigent or underprivileged."

"She could identify solutions within the law and implement her ideas," said Jennifer Jergens, a law school classmate. "When she did something, she did it well."

Maxwell and Davenport had recently begun dating.

"Just the other day Tony told me how crazy he was about her," Jablonski said. "We all felt like she could accomplish anything she set her mind to. She was a very organized, methodical person."

Davenport, a 1986 graduate of Frontier High School in Hamburg, was completing a master's degree in English education at Buffalo State College and spent the past two years substituting in local high schools. His goal was to become a full-time teacher.

"Kids loved him when he came here," said Keefe, South Park High School's principal. "He was a big burly guy who had a gentleness with our students. Several used to stop me in the halls and request Mr. D. to be their sub."

Whether playing guitar, tossing a Frisbee or barbequing on the grill, Davenport embraced life with a positive outlook.

Tuesday night, after learning of the tragedy, friends gathered at a Main Street bar where Davenport sometimes went.

By 9:30, it was crowded with acquaintances of the three victims.

"I looked around and saw so many familiar faces," Jablonski said. "The three of them were young, but this turnout proves they influenced so many lives."

Many friends viewed the accident as cruel fate.

"News reports are saying that area of ice off Fort Erie can be unpredictable," Jablonski noted. "If they had gone twenty feet left or right, we'd probably all be sitting here laughing about it."

25

Senior Tactical Flight Officer Daniel L. Vargas shared more than just a cockpit with Captain McClusky. In many ways he was a carbon copy of his boss — only more intense. Ten years younger, he learned aviation with the Army, serving nearly two decades, including a stint in Iraq during the Gulf War. Short, lean, muscular, his dark hair was a thin crew cut.

McClusky was shy in groups, but Vargas turned mute. When first arriving at the Sheriff's office, he was nicknamed "Marcel," as in Marcel Marceau, the French mime. No one argued that he was steady, reliable, and extremely bright. Yet his propensity for silence unnerved co-workers. He would walk into a room and nod rather than say hello. Two months into the job, one of the younger deputies secretly kept surveillance on Vargas for an entire workday, and by quitting time deemed the flight officer had spoken twenty-four words during his eight-hour shift. "That boils down to three words an hour," the deputy reported gleefully. "Amazing when you realize I've probably just said twenty-four words in my last two sentences."

Immature perhaps. But the men he worked with were less clever than they imagined. On the day when he spoke only twenty-four words, Vargas had been nursing a case of laryngitis, so he had not planned to talk much anyway. Yet early in his shift he overheard a deputy outside his door whispering the plan to track Vargas' speech. Vargas grinned to himself, vowing to remain in his office whenever possible. By the end of the shift, he was disappointed he had to talk at all.

Vargas, for his part, found nothing unusual in his habits of speech. Why speak if a gesture will suffice? he reasoned. If I have something to say, others will hear it. Otherwise, best to keep it zipped. One of his favorite old clichés seemed wise: It's better to remain silent and be thought a fool than to open your mouth and remove any doubt. He was amused by a tale about President Calvin Coolidge, known as "Silent Cal." Once, at a party, a man approached him and said, "I bet my wife I could get you to say three words." Coolidge paused before replying, "You lose."

McClusky had hired Vargas three years earlier, when his original partner retired. He sensed the two would compliment each other, and was not adverse to gaps of silence. The need to constantly talk, McClusky believed, exposed a character flaw of inferiority. As they grew familiar and months stretched to years, Vargas lost shyness. There were no longer any inhibitions, but his cadence remained measured, each word carefully thought out.

McClusky respected such deliberation: flying a helicopter was a perpetual risk. A cautious co-pilot often was the difference between a successful rescue and losing a victim.

* * *

For Captain David McClusky, recurring dreams were triggered by the daytime search. They continued steadily for several weeks. Nightmares of being trapped on ice were so vivid, so real and crisp, that he was assured of imminent death. His chest seized with disbelief. In the hazy line between wakefulness and subconscious, McClusky was unable to grasp the false logic of these visions, remaining trapped inside them, surrounded by a shrinking plexiglass bubble. Escape was not an option. Terror was real…

A cold morning, long ago. Megan was only three years old, a tot who stood to his upper leg. Her knit mitten grasped his gloved fingers. She wore a pink overcoat, white faux fur rimming its hood, and dark nylon snow pants that made a shishing noise as her stubby legs moved. Rubber boots were soundless as they stepped. She was too light to create a crunching noise against snow.

Although his daughter was sharply focused, edges of his vision were blurred like melted cellophane. With the impact of a collision, McClusky suddenly realized they were atop Lake Erie's crusted ice, its luster a reflecting faded jade, where the cliffs of Hamburg's shore stretched before him several hundred yards away. His heartbeat quickened. He knew inherent dangers and had preached against this. His own voice echoed through a lecture hall: there is no such thing as safe ice. Instinctively, he arched his legs wider. He wanted to pick up his daughter, cradle her against his chest, protect her from peril. But that would increase his weight. Megan, lighter than he, was less likely to puncture through if she stood on her own. She would be safer away from him.

Don't panic. Think.

"Sweetie," he said, releasing her hand. "Listen to daddy now. Do you want to play a game?"

She nodded with vigor.

"Good," he continued. "Here's how it works. First off, no running. You walk behind me a little bit, but you're only allowed to step where I've stepped. And you can't get too close. If you see my footprints, it's okay to walk there. But don't walk anywhere else, okay?"

"What do I get if I win?" she asked.

You get to live, he thought. This is more than just a game — losing could mean death. Please, dear God, don't let my daughter die on Lake Erie. Guide us safely to shore.

McClusky's footsteps were slow, deliberate. He contemplated each step, alert for air bubbles, discoloration, cracked edges — any sign of weakened ice. Behind him, Megan chided "faster," proclaiming, "this is fun, daddy!"

Although time consuming, the first 200 yards were safe. But as McClusky drew nearer to land, he saw ice in the distance thinned and vanished, opening upon a visible stream parallel to shore. It dribbled like a twisting blue krait in both directions. Beyond was solid ice again. The stream was narrow — only five or six feet, depending on its ebbing edges — but still too wide to leap. Besides, ice adjacent to water would be tender, unsafe. McClusky stopped twenty feet from the brook, halting in place. Megan, six feet behind her father, kept a steady distance, miming his pivots as he surveyed both directions for a solid bridge to shore.

There must be a safe route, McClusky thought. If we made it out here, certainly there is a way back. But because he could not remember venturing onto the lake — why had he been so stupid? — there was no way to retrace his steps. He scoured the shore for familiar sights, buildings or terrain which might provide a compass. The landscape was just outside his scope of understanding. Nothing made sense.

"Daddy, why did we stop?"

"Let's go this way, honey," McClusky said, turning left to continue the trek. "Remember, only step where I step."

Her three-year old voice was tinged with annoyance. "I know how to play the game!"

They trekked further, McClusky leading the way, gingerly, scanning all directions for a connection to land. Yet the stream continued to snake through the lake, twisting without interruption.

McClusky's thoughts turned toward a viable alternative plan. *If I had a ladder, I could lay it across the stream to crawl over. Maybe I could find a substitute out here — an abandoned tree trunk, perhaps. Heck, if Megan wasn't with me, I would even risk leaping it. If I broke through, and could not pull myself out, I'm close enough to shore that I could break off ice chunks and wade toward land. But I can't do that now. Not with my daughter. She will not remain alone out here, no matter what.*

"Why are we stopping again?" Megan asked.

"Daddy needs to think."

While he studied land, hoping someone would materialize on the bluffs to notice their predicament, Megan remained several feet from her father, but began dancing, shimmying her shoulders and hips like the cartoon characters she watched each Saturday morning. Noticing her joyful dance with his peripheral vision, a quote leaped into McClusky's head: "If you're going to walk on thin ice, you might as well dance." It had been printed on bathroom wallpaper at a friend's house. The metaphor might have been clever, but its literal interpretation advertised ignorance.

Megan's bouncing hips moved to the left. Before McClusky could warn her to stand still, ice opened with a thunderclapping shhuuummm and swallowed her completely.

Immediately, he sat bolt upright in bed, sweat-soaked and bone-weary. The room was humid, blankets thick with perspiration. He stifled the heavy exhale which crawled from his stomach.

* * *

Friday, February 25, 1994 | 8:23 a.m.

McClusky checked the day's weather forecast. Morning would remain cold, but winds slowed overnight so that navigating Sky One could be done safely. Three days of high gusts and plunging temperatures had kept them grounded. Such conditions made it difficult to predict what ice formations would look like near Fort Erie.

I should have been a meteorologist, McClusky thought, creasing the printout. Weathermen claim to be scientists, but they're wrong more often than not. No one seems to give a damn.

Seemingly half awake, Danny Vargas stumbled through the hangar door, his cheeks and eyes exposed beneath a knit cap. Removing gloves, he raised hands to his mouth and exhaled warm breath into balled fists. He looked at McClusky with expectation.

"Morning, Cap," he said. "Got a weather report?"

"Winds are dying," McClusky answered, raising the typewritten sheet as proof. "I think we can make a go of it today."

"Let me grab some coffee, then I'll suit up."

"Yeah, let's hit it. We've lost three days."

Vargas paused uncomfortably, removing his hat and running palms across the brush cut, as if short hair could be disheveled. "Listen Cap… you know the odds are pretty long here, right?"

McClusky said nothing.

"It's been six days," Vargas continued. "Those bodies are on the lake bottom, and by now they may have moved. If the Coast Guard can't find them with the underwater camera, the odds of us spotting anything from air is…"

"I know, Danny," McClusky barked testily. Images from his most recent nightmare hovered behind his eyes. "But we owe it to them. It's our job."

Vargas looked repentant, as if his words conveyed too much subtext. His partner had taken this search and recovery to heart — moreso than any Vargas could recall. He worried about its effect on McClusky's psyche.

"I know that, Cap. I really do." Vargas released a breath. "I just don't want to see you get all worked up then mope around with disappointment if we don't find anything."

McClusky's sternness faded. He exhaled a confession. "I'm pretty sure that if we haven't found them by this afternoon, orders are going to come down to stop looking. I don't blame the boss — hell, this is probably a fool's errand — but I'd sure like to find them before that happens."

Vargas nodded sympathetically. "Okay. So let me pour a cup of joe and we'll get moving."

* * *

Buffalo News: Sunday, February 27, 1994. Page B1, local section

DANGERS OF HIKING LAKE ERIE
DOOMED INEXPERIENCED TRIO
Current likely to blame for drownings

Temperature warmed to a near record 63 degrees as three

friends set out to cross Lake Erie on Feb. 19 — and they were in danger from the moment they left Hamburg Beach.

Thin ice was their downfall, but air temperature was only a minor factor, according to experts.

Even if it had been below freezing, ice near Crescent Beach — their target destination on the Ontario shore — is notoriously dangerous.

It was not warm sunshine, but "rotting ice" from below that doomed Anthony Davenport, 25, Victoria Maxwell, 26, and Amy Black, 28. The three Buffalo residents are presumed to have fallen through ice and drowned since they went missing more than a week ago.

"It is never safe to cross Lake Erie," said Capt. David McClusky, who leads the search and rescue operations for the Erie County Sheriff's Department. "No matter how cold it is, the lake is just too unpredictable. I would never advocate walking across because there's no path that guarantees safety."

Despite the long winter of ice buildup and lake temperature hovering just above the freezing mark, currents from below can cause "rot," especially if they are fed by warmer stream runoffs. Thus, with warm sunshine above, the ice was being attacked from both sides.

"Lake Erie has a fast current running through it," said Arnold SanFillippo, president of the Lake Erie Fisherman's Council. "People think of the lake as tranquil, and it appears to be, but if you don't understand and respect the patterns, it can be deadly."

No path across the lake is safe to walk, according to experts, but the route chosen by three friends was particularly dangerous. In the past several years, two snowmobilers drowned and an ice fisherman was rescued from the same two-square-mile area of bay near Crescent Beach.

"It's still not safe, but they would have had a greater likelihood of success if they had gone further west, toward Point Abino," McClusky said.

Still, there is no guarantee of solid ice, even when the surface appears strong.

From Sky One, the Sheriff's Department helicopter, McClusky has seen cracks in the ice travel quickly as wind speed increased. Ice fishermen — or anyone on the lake — can become trapped, cut off from land.

SanFillippo, an expert on Lake Erie ice patterns, said there are many misconceptions about weather conditions affecting the lake.

The trio departed from Hamburg Town Park Beach, a well-protected area with little current. Ice that day was 18 inches thick, and there was little hint of coming danger.

"Hamburg Beach can be deceptive," SanFillippo said. "You stand there and look across toward Canada, and it seems much closer than it is. If it's sunny, all you get is a glaring reflection of white. There is no way to tell where weak spots are."

It would appear that people could walk across ice without risk, confident they could spot trouble ahead.

Not true, according to McClusky.

"Even someone with a trained eye would have trouble detecting exactly where the weak spots are," McClusky said. "There's often no way of telling visually how strong ice is. Your first sign anything is wrong would be when you broke through."

Once that happens, survival is possible — provided the victim has the proper equipment. Life preservers, ropes and a hand spike would be vital. The spike — a block of wood with a protruding nail point — could be driven into ice from below and used by the person who fell through to pull himself out.

It is unknown whether the trio brought along any lifesaving supplies.

Even with such equipment, a rescue would be difficult. Cold water would sap the victim's energy within minutes.

"There aren't many people who break through ice and survive," McClusky noted.

Although no bodies have been recovered, a green jacket was spotted approximately one-half mile from the Canadian shore amid a field of open holes. Shifting ice has made it difficult to determine exactly where the hikers fell through. The search was suspended earlier in the week due to poor weather conditions, but McClusky is determined to complete the task.

"I'm fairly certain that the bodies are sunk within a few feet of where they went in," he said. "It's just a matter of pinpointing the right area. We know a general location of where they are, and for the families' sake, we want to recover the bodies as soon as we can."

26

In the winter of 1964, the New York Power Authority
and Ontario Hydro, having formed an International Joint
Commission, began yearly installation of an ice boom at the
mouth of Lake Erie. The ice boom is a series of connected
logs stretching in a shallow arc more than a mile and a half,
at the point where the lake narrows into Niagara River.
Spanning the outer breakwall from Buffalo Harbor almost to
the Canadian shore, sections are anchored to the lake's bottom at 400-foot intervals.

Its purpose is to promote early solidification of a naturally
occurring ice bridge in the lake's eastern basin. This retaining
wall helps to reduce icebergs flowing downriver which could
damage property, docks and hydropower intakes during
winter and early spring. It also decreases the chance of local
flooding by keeping ice bottled on the expansive lake instead
of filtering into the river.

The International Joint Commission decreed that the ice
boom be installed each year when Lake Erie's temperature
falls to thirty-nine degrees Fahrenheit (four degrees Celsius)

or on December 16, whichever comes first. Two hundred eighty-six logs, each weighing one and a half tons, measuring thirty feet long, sixteen inches high and twenty-two inches wide, stretch across the lake in twenty-two separate sections. (In 2000, a new millennium saw logs replaced by steel cylinders with slightly different measurements). The complex process of rigging the ice boom takes between three and five days, assuming there are no weather interruptions.

Secured in place, current flows unimpeded under the ice boom. If pressure buildup is too great, the boom submerges so ice cakes can spill over. Floatation returns the logs to the surface after pressure is eased. Because the ice boom does not cross the entire width of lake, there is no structural barrier for watercraft, which are able to navigate around either end as needed.

Statistically, a normal winter sees more than 8,000 square miles of ice crust across Lake Erie, most of which melts in place as spring approaches. The ice boom is removed only when the frozen surface area shrinks below 250 square miles, as measured by aerial surveys. Removal dates vary each year, but most often fall sometime in April.

There have been rare winters when Lake Erie has not frozen. This phenomenon occurred in 1953, 1983, and later, in 2002. Prior to the international agreement that initiated an ice boom, New York Power Authority and Ontario Hydro used icebreakers to minimize buildup in the river.

Although it has been in place for several decades, the ice boom remains controversial. Opponents argue that its presence alters the climate in Western New York. Creation of a man-made ice bridge keeps the lake colder than it would naturally be, complainants allege, delaying spring in the region. Meteorologists agree that warm weather may arrive later than people like, but offer evidence that the bridge would form naturally without the boom, and its presence allows for greater control of nature's uncertainties. Prevailing southwesterly winds, weather experts say, are to blame for late thaws. Others cite a negative affect on spring fishing season. In 1983, the Panel on Niagara River Ice Boom Investigations discounted those claims, saying there was no significant alteration to local fisheries or recreational angling.

A nearby restaurant has attempted to capitalize on the ice boom's removal, offering daily specials during "Boom Days." Local papers run columns that chronicle the boom's installation each winter and subsequent removal the following spring. Visible from the Peace Bridge's apex, the ice boom is a regional novelty, an anomaly which has unseen impact on people's lives.

* * *

On Thursday, April 21, 1994, almost three decades after its first annual installation, workers on a tugboat began detaching anchors and removing the ice boom's logs from the position they had held since the previous December 16. On the lake's surface, cascading flow altered the stagnant buildup of ice. Chunks that remained bottled in the basin's mouth rumbled and collided against neighboring icebergs, pushing ahead anxiously towards an aperture where they could rush into the river, freed from restraint. Downstream, ice backed up, impeding water flow through intakes for Ontario Hydro and New York Power Authority plants. By Monday, April 25, only nine of the twenty-two boom sections had been removed, and the International Joint Commission agreed to delay the process until more ice melted.

In rocky shallows east of Crescent Beach sprawled three corpses, sunken since February. The bodies were not anchored or snagged, yet they had remained in place for weeks, undulating in a slow corkscrew motion like free-floating seaweed. Cold had preserved the dead. Still, time eroded signs of life: faces and limbs hung down; chests grew bloated. Beneath gloved hands, fingernails had loosened, beginning to peel away. Eyeballs shriveled, exposing hollow sockets. Although the process was retarded by frigid water, Amy Black, Tony Davenport and Victoria Maxwell were disintegrating, vanishing secretly under a slate of ice. Their submerged corpses remained elusive to all but the eyes of God.

Removal of the ice boom's logs and the ensuing backup into the river triggered subtle current shifts on the rocky lake floor, which in turn provoked movement of the corpses. Silently, gracefully, like a ballet dancer without an audience, Amy Black's decaying physique was drawn from shore, down the lake bed's incline, away from her friends toward the deepening crater. Over time, in miniscule increments, water flow forced the body into the funnel of Niagara River.

Tony Davenport's limpid form inched ahead as well. His corpse crept several feet from its resting spot, hanging wrists and palms dragging against the rocky lake bottom like a knife scraping darkened toast. Over the course of three days, he drifted two dozen feet, shifting to and from shore in almost imperceptible segments. The movement would have continued, but on the third day, motion was halted when the body snagged against an obstruction — the lifeless bulk of Victoria Maxwell.

Her mouth was chiseled open, frozen flesh stretching loosely from her cheeks, body inverted so Victoria's feet aimed heavenward. When Tony's frame bumped hers, the action shifted her shoulders, and slowly the corpse twisted into a helix like an astronaut tumbling through zero gravity. The gentle collision dislodged a canvas backpack that was still looped into the crook of her elbow.

The pack fluttered free, sunk and began creeping away. Tony's body pushed against Victoria's, where their lifeless forms merged into one — a silent, final embrace. Thus time supplied what life could not — a union of two lovers that would last forever as their melded bodies disintegrated into decay.

27

"Things have slowed down," Carly Cain said to the store's owner, Maria. "I'm so dog-tired I could sleep on this cash register. Any problem if I go on break now?"

Maria smiled dumbly, saying Carly's cheek would look mottled with indentations from register keys. That would be bad for customers to see, so she should step away. Have her dinner break and be back in a half hour. Carly didn't appreciate the silly smile — she considered fleetingly that the older woman was somehow mocking her haggard appearance — nor did she know the meaning of "mottled." She thought Maria said "modeled" and did not understand the attempt at humor. Even had she grasped the homonym, Carly was too fatigued to think of anything except going outside for a cigarette and pressing her eyelids together. The half hour break could be stretched to forty minutes. It was enough time to squeeze in a power nap.

A plate glass window overlooked the widened road, where Carly's battered Chevy Impala was parked at an angle before the sidewalk. When she began working there, six months

ago, Carly could not understand how a small shop sell-
ing porcelain figurines and miniature stuffed animals could
survive in this two block area of Fort Erie. It was a mix of
commercial and residential properties, but its only draw was
the Niagara River at the bottom of the hill. More often than
not, the neighborhood was deserted. The Peace Bridge, link-
ing Canada to Buffalo, was several blocks south, but tourists
rarely strayed from the connecting highways — they simply
wanted to cross the bridge. There were frequent days when
the cash register's total intake equaled zero. Often, it cost
more money to open the shop than it would to remain dark.
Carly considered suggesting that Maria should relocate up
the road, closer to Niagara Falls. That area was a tourist trap.
But Carly was only twenty-one, earning a pittance at this
crummy job anyway. Why would a business owner listen to
anything she had to offer?

Carly cranked down the car windows, removed a pack of
cigarettes from the glove compartment, and lit one quickly,
inhaling smoke with an addict's relief. She had been bar-
hopping with friends the night before, arriving home close to
sunrise. The plan had been to sleep late into the afternoon,
and she was coherent enough last night to set the alarm for
3 p.m., which left ample time to shower and dry her hair before the four o'clock shift began. Carly did not count on the
teenager across the street setting up his new drum kit in the
garage that faced her window. At 11 that morning, he had
begun attacking the bass and snare like he was wrestling an
uncontrolled jackhammer. Carly's hangover pounded in time
with the beat.

Now fatigue had seeped marrow deep, and her skin felt
lumpy, coated with clay. Through the muddy haze of Marl-
boro smoke, Carly could sense the coming summer. A week

earlier had been Victoria Day — the May "two four" cel-
ebration — and that got her thinking about beach volleyball
and outdoor barbeques. Tonight air was thick and humid,
like breathing through a wet cotton sweater. She sat in the
driver's seat and fumbled for the latch to recline. Too damn
muggy. Cooler on the river, she thought, and if I go there
Maria won't be able to stare me down through the picture
window. She returned the chair to its upright position and
turned over the ignition.

The shoreline was only a block away, at the hill's bottom. There was a parking area dimpled with craters in the
packed earth, a spillover lot for the strip club across the
street. Carly descended the incline slowly, watching a short,
chunky blonde wearing a miniskirt and high heels approach
the club's back door. The area was mostly vacant — perverts
wouldn't be coming to ogle the women until after dark, even
if the strippers arrived now — so she pulled the Impala behind the protection of looming elm trees and patches of field
grass. Already it seemed cooler here, even though it was only
a few hundred yards from the shop. She had a private view of
the river, isolated enough that no one would disturb her.

Carly knew this area well. Niagara Boulevard, clinging to
the river's shore between the Peace Bridge and Niagara Falls,
was dotted with small parkland retreats which abutted the
water. Some had paved areas large enough for a dozen cars;
others were tiny, able to fit only three. Trees overhung the
banks, and wooden picnic tables were strategically placed
within view of water. In high school, Carly and her friends
had driven the parkway and counted: twenty-eight picnic
areas along the length of the twenty-kilometer highway.
Depending on the night, they brought beer to various alcoves
as the sun fell, appreciating springtime and the privacy of the

river.

To Carly's right was the blackened steel lattice of the old International Railroad Bridge, spanning two countries with girders that crouched close to the current. The bridge was a series of oversized trapezoids whose base angles linked together. The viaduct had been constructed low intentionally as railroad barons tried to outmuscle the shipping industry on the Niagara River. If goods could not pass under the connector, the logic went, they would need to be shipped over it.

Carly tossed her cigarette out the window. Beside her car, the stub smoldered, emitting wisps of transparent smoke. Only feet from the river, she was again surprised at how quickly its current surged. Driving parallel to it, or crossing from the height of the Peace Bridge, one did not notice the speed of water. But sitting at eye level, she could relish its rapid flow, right to left, and savor the raw power. It was majestic, she thought, a force greater than anything humans could create. How many nights had she partied along the shore and taken this for granted?

The humid breeze, the cigarette, being unchained from the counter… Carly felt more awake. She inhaled deeply, tasting spring in the back of her throat, excited that daylight lingered until nearly 9 o'clock. Take a quick walk, get your body moving again, she thought. After a few lungfuls of humid air to dilute the nicotine, her system would feel cleansed — and then she could lie down.

To the left a small peninsula jutted twenty feet into the river, making an abrupt turn toward the current. Several maturing elms stretched upward, leaning away from packed soil. The elbow of land sheltered an inlet, calm and shallow enough that Carly could see the rocky bottom through mocha-colored water. A corrugated drainage pipe, covered by an earthen bridge, let the buildup escape the bay's backside. She ventured onto the peninsula, toward lapping water. Boulders lay at its thrust edge to buffer erosion. In the irregular gaps between riprap was a collection of junk: an empty soda can, a crushed cardboard cigarette box, two crumbled plastic potato chip wrappers and a dead seagull with scraggily black and white feathers, body plump as a cat. Carly drew her head away and studied the far shore.

From here, much of Buffalo's view was camouflaged by trees, but a church steeple pointed skyward. Carly knew the landscape: to the right, obstructed by the railroad bridge, were the taller buildings of downtown. On the left was a yacht club.

Seagulls squawked behind her. She pivoted and watched a flock hanging above the current, flapping against the breeze without appearing to move, hooked beaks opening and closing. One particularly aggressive gull lowered its head and dove toward bristles of shrubs overhanging the shore. Scavenging for food, its neck submerged near a black log bobbing a few feet from the bank.

Wonder where that stump came from, Carly thought. Had it passed through other Great Lakes and filtered this far downriver? How long had it been submerged? Would it ever dislodge and leave this tiny inlet, or simply decay here as years passed?

Funny, Carly noticed, but the end of the flotsam protruded a few inches, almost like a shoe pointing skyward. The log rolled gently from side to side, like the slow tentativeness of a drunk struggling for balance. For such a thick trunk, its length was short — between five or six feet. Somewhere its ends must have sheared away.

But damn, that nub looked like a blackened shoe. It was

rounded perfectly and — Carly stepped onto one of the boulders and leaned forward, narrowing her gaze — there almost seemed to be a contoured toe poking up. As the log twisted away, Carly could not be sure. Was it a tree at all?

A sudden fear clenched her. It began in the back of her neck and flashed downward, tightness gripping her chest. She trotted from the peninsula back to shore, pulse racing. There would be a better view from the other side. Could it be? On the bank's incline, she pushed aside grasses and weeds, craning her neck above the bramble. Water was the color of creamy tea, but from five feet away, there was no mistaking the winter boots, dark pants and black wool sweater. Floating just below the water line, facial features were rotted away, leaving only a charcoal smear where eyes and mouth had been.

It was a waking nightmare that Carly Cain would never forget. The moment she realized it was a body, she leaped back, opened her mouth to scream, and tasted bile rising in her throat. Without stopping, she vomited on the lawn, scurrying inland, away from the river, as if chased by an invisible madman.

* * *

Buffalo News: Wednesday, June 1, 1994. Local section, p. B1.

BODY FOUND IN NIAGARA RIVER
MAY BE MISSING BUFFALO MAN

Authorities are trying to determine whether a body discovered along the Niagara River shoreline Tuesday was that of a missing Buffalo man presumed drowned in Lake Erie during the winter.

The body of a man dressed in winter clothing was found near the International Railroad Bridge yesterday evening.

Niagara Regional Police said they suspect the body may be that of Anthony Davenport, 25, of Buffalo. He and two female companions have been missing and presumed drowned since they attempted to walk across the frozen lake on Feb. 19.

"We have no other missing persons in the area," said Niagara Regional Police Sgt. Ellis Chamberlain. "We can't be sure it's him, but the possibility is in the back of our minds."

An autopsy will be performed today at Hamilton General Hospital.

Carly Cain, 21, of Fort Erie, discovered the body in the early evening just north of the International Railroad Bridge.

The body appeared to be that of a white male with dark hair, although authorities said it was difficult to estimate an age due to decomposition. Police said it appeared to have been in the water for some time.

The body was dressed in a black wool sweater, dark pants and winter boots.

Also missing and presumed drowned are Amy Black, 28, of Fort Erie, and Victoria Maxwell, 26, of Buffalo.

* * *

Buffalo News: Saturday, June 4, 1994. Front page.

BODY DISCOVERED ON CANADIAN SHORE IDENTIFIED

A body discovered washed up on the banks of the Niagara River last Tuesday has been identified as one of three friends presumed drowned after attempting to walk across ice-covered Lake Erie last February.

Niagara Regional Police identified the body as that of Amy Black, 28, who had addresses in both Buffalo and Fort Erie, Ont. Positive identification was finalized yesterday through dental records.

Originally, the decomposed body was thought to be male. Authorities said there was no sign of foul play in Ms. Black's death.

Ms. Black departed from Hamburg Beach on Feb. 19 with two friends, Anthony Davenport, 25, and Victoria Maxwell, 26, both of Buffalo. The three were reported missing two days later when none of them could be found at home or their jobs.

The other two bodies have not been located.

28

Again, butterflies.

Capt. David McClusky gave himself a pep talk: I've taught this before. I know my subject. These kids are eager to learn; they approach the job with sincerity and respect. There is nothing to be nervous about.

Still...

His daughter Megan must have inherited the teaching gene from Molly's side, sure as hell not his. Last night, he updated notes, made copies and checked overhead transparencies, then couldn't fall asleep until 3 a.m. — despite being fully prepared. Adding insult, McClusky was too jittery to eat breakfast this morning. I'm as nervous as a whore in church, and all for no reason other than I hate the first two minutes of this job.

"You'll be fine," Molly told him as he left the house. "Relax. Think of the fun we're going to have next week at Thanksgiving."

"Yeah. Me and the in-laws. It'll be a blast."

She swatted him playfully. Feelings were warm between

David and Molly's parents, but that never stopped him from teasing. "Two can play that game, you know. With your brother giving the blessing, I'll have to be on best behavior."

David said dryly, "Swore like a sailor when he was a kid. Now he's a priest."

"Imagine our families gathered around the table, and your nerves will vanish." Molly winked and nuzzled his neck. "Extra candied yams if you do a good job today."

He raised an eyebrow. "I'm a sucker for candied yams."

"Or you're just a sucker."

"For doing this job, I think I am."

* * *

With initial fear evaporated, McClusky's voice commanded the lecture hall. Only minutes in, he had already garnered respect from these recruits.

"Last winter we had a situation that got some media attention," McClusky said. "You probably heard about it. Three people in their mid-twenties — just about your age — thought it would be fun to hike across the lake. It was a warm day, but they were convinced there was no danger. Sunshine can weaken a surface, and ice can rot from below as well, no matter how cold it is outside. Things we are going to talk about today — like uneven depths, stream runoffs, and current — are all culprits. These young people unknowingly ventured into a two-square-mile area near Crescent Beach that is notorious for trouble.

"The distance they intended to cover was approximately ten miles. They almost made it. During the search, from the helicopter my partner and I spotted openings in the ice and a partially submerged jacket about a half-mile from shore.

They were about ten minutes from reaching land when they went in."

Beginning at the nearest desk, McClusky passed out photocopies of the Buffalo News article from February 23, in which reporter Janet Long profiled the victims. During the pause, trainees were silent as eyes absorbed the words.

"For the record, the victims' names were Anthony Davenport, Victoria Maxwell, and Amy Black. I never met them, but in some ways, I feel like I know them. By the time I got the missing persons call, it was too late for rescue, but I spent several days searching for their remains. I was not successful in finding their bodies, and that bothers me. I say their names to remind you that these are real people who lost their lives. The article in front of you helps to illustrate that. Three people gone because of poor decision-making.

"Do I wish they had been smarter? You're damn right. They had no training or preparation for such an excursion, and they didn't even take basic safety precautions. All three were college graduates who should have known better. The article suggests they were good people who contributed to the community in positive ways. Unfortunately, as this incident illustrates, anyone can make poor choices.

"As a law enforcement official, you can learn from this incident. Choices you make can be critical, and can have ramifications for those we serve and protect.

"For years I've stood on a soapbox and harangued about the dangers of ice and the need for caution. Yet every year, people get stranded there and sometimes die before we can rescue them. A cynic would say it's job security for me, but I don't think that way. When I'm involved in a recovery like this one, I feel like I'm preaching in Siberia on a windy day."

29

Wednesday, July 26, 2000 | 9:51 a.m.

Captain David McClusky's office was small enough that he
sarcastically referred to it as "the closet." Its cinderblock walls
were coated with a neutral-colored industrial paint. There
was just enough square footage for a desk and chair on either
side. Tacked to the wall, two corkboards were an overflow-
ing minefield papers and photos. A narrow window was the
room's only redeeming feature. When he felt claustrophobic,
McClusky would slide it open and gaze westward toward
oncoming weather.

His colleagues ribbed him about the tiny cubical: You've
been here more than thirty years, Cap, and this is the best
they can do for you? But McClusky never complained about
his closet. Smaller area meant less to clean, and he preferred
to spend most of his time in the hangar or Sky One anyway.

Now, on a humid Wednesday morning, a newspaper was
spread across McClusky's desk. He leaned forward to skim
its words. Raising a coffee cup, he absently blew a cooling
breath against the rim. The phone rang, but he did not divert
eyes as he lifted the receiver.

"McClusky," he said curtly.

"Yeah, Captain… this is Deputy Angelo Campagna from Grand Island." The voice paused, anticipating recognition. "We've met a few times over the years."

In addition to being the largest island in the Niagara River, Grand Island was one of only three suburbs that did not have a local police force. The county sheriff's department ran a substation there, assuming law-enforcement responsibilities for the community. Giant trellised bridges on both its north and south end connected the island to Niagara Falls and Buffalo.

McClusky recognized the name, but hesitated, scanning his memory. "Angelo… yeah. You ride patrol with Wally Matthews, right?"

The voice sounded relieved. "That's it."

"Sure, I remember you. How's old Wally doing?"

"Yeah, he's good," Campagna replied. "I don't know when you spoke to him last, but he and the wife had another little girl last spring."

"Oh, that's great. Give him my regards."

"I will."

"How about you? You doing all right?"

"Yeah, working hard, you know?"

"Last time I saw you, there was a cast on your wrist, right?" McClusky asked.

"Huh… I guess so. That was three years ago. Good memory."

"So what's up?" McClusky wondered.

"I've got something here I think you're going to be interested in."

"Shoot."

"Couple of divers were fooling around yesterday near a

pier in the Niagara River. In the east branch, over by the Holiday Inn. They're not far from shore. Shallow water, ten or twelve feet deep. One of them submerges and spots a backpack resting on the river bottom. It's got some silt covering it, but looks to be in pretty good shape. So they haul it up, open it on shore, and find ID. One of the divers recognizes a name from that case of yours a couple years ago, and brings it to the station."

McClusky stopped scanning the newspaper. He was interested now. "Which case?" he asked, straightening posture.

"Those kids who walked across Lake Erie. I think this backpack belonged to one of them."

"Yeah? Which one?"

"Victoria Maxwell. Is that one of the names?"

"It sure is," McClusky answered.

"That's crazy," Campagna laughed. "I'm looking at her student ID card from the University at Buffalo. When the heck was that, anyway?"

* * *

Wednesday, July 26, 2000 | 4:57 p.m.

A storm front moved eastward, aiming directly at McClusky's office window. He had propped feet on the edge of his waste can, twirled a rubber band through his thumb and forefinger, and stared toward approaching clouds. They were dark gray, filled with ominous hints. Great mood for a Vincent Price movie, McClusky thought. Afternoon had been sticky. When rain finally came — he was certain droplets would begin falling within minutes — he hoped humidity would wash away.

McClusky had spent much of the day visiting the past.

After talking to Campagna, he pulled old case files on Anthony Davenport, Amy Black and Victoria Maxwell. It had been almost six and a half years since that search, and there were elements about it that still troubled him. He and Vargas had been in Sky One that day, on routine patrol. How had they missed three kids when they passed over the lake? It was sunny, clear, and visibility stretched for miles. And why in hell hadn't they been able to locate those bodies immediately following their disappearance? Yes, weather and geography were factors. But he had spotted the girl's down vest on the ice field. If that was where they went under, their bodies couldn't have traveled far.

But no one could find them. Not his partner's keen eyes, nor technology. With an assist from the Coast Guard, they had used the grappling hook, underwater cameras, the infrared… all to no avail.

It must not have been where they went under. That's the determination he made back in 1994. Amy Black must have discarded her jacket away from the spot that she drowned. Why? What happened out there to cause that? Did her jacket get pulled below into current and surface in a different spot? Months later, Amy Black's body was discovered in the Niagara River near the railroad bridge. Currents were unpredictable, of course, but who would expect Victoria Maxwell's backpack to be found miles downstream, past that spot?

McClusky's thoughts were interrupted when Danny Vargas poked his head through the doorway.

"What do you say, Cap? Ready to knock off for the day?"

McClusky lowered his feet. "No… the deputy from Grand Island said he was going to bring me that backpack on his way home. I thought he'd be here by now."

"Have him leave it at the front desk. It'll be here

tomorrow."

"I'd rather wait."

"Want me to stick around?"

"Nah," McClusky said, waving a friendly hand. "Get out of here. Maybe you can beat the rain."

When Campagna finally arrived, closer to 5:30, he and McClusky shook hands. The deputy was older than McClusky recalled, and had added fifteen pounds. They chatted briefly in the lobby, but there was little to say that they hadn't discussed earlier on the phone. Campagna, dripping from rain, appeared anxious to get home.

Campagna handed McClusky a black plastic garbage bag knotted at the top.

"The backpack is in here," he said. "After you go through it you don't mind calling the family to return stuff?"

In the files was a phone number for Maxwell's parents in Toledo. He had noticed it earlier, wondering if those digits were still valid. McClusky was reluctant to make such a call. Who knew if the family still lived there? And the larger questions: how did their daughter's death affect her mother and father? McClusky imaged that walking past her empty room on the way downstairs to breakfast every morning would be a torment. The Maxwells probably sold the house, relocated. Did they remain together, or did this tragedy rip apart their marriage, send them skittering in different directions, to different states, seeking a solace that might never come? Tracking them down could be a challenge. Selfishly, McClusky did not want to wrap himself in sordid tales or crumbled lives. Further, after all the effort expended to locate Victoria's parents, maybe news that her effects had been recovered would cause their slow healing to regress. Hell, McClusky thought, I'm a parent. How could you ever really heal if one of your kids died?

"I guess I could," McClusky said. "Is there anything they would want?"

"Doubt it. A few personal effects. I thought you'd care to see it, anyway."

"I'm glad you called," McClusky said, offering a hand to shake. "Really appreciate it."

Campagana left, and the station resumed its quiet. Mc-Clusky lugged the package to his office, plopping it on his desk. Beads of rain slid down the crumpled sides, dappling the blotter. He loosened the knot, lifting the sack from within, depositing the wet garbage bag into the waste can.

Canvas was olive green, with an American flag stitched to its flap. Edges showed hints of fray, but seams and shoulder loops remained intact. Years of submersion in cold water had preserved the backpack well.

McClusky tingled, feeling a chill beneath his skin. This was spooky, the stuff of ghosts. He never met Victoria Maxwell, but felt an unspoken kinship. He had a flashbulb memory of days spent searching, the ensuing media attention. Still, all these years later, an occasional nightmare about being lost on the lake muddled his sleep.

He considered where Victoria's body might have ended up. Had she removed the backpack from her shoulders before submersion? If not, how did it get separated from her? Did the corpse disintegrate around it? That was unlikely. Did crabs or other scavengers pluck away at flesh and bone until there was nothing left? If so, might her clothes have been nearby?

So damn many questions, he thought. There would be no answers. This backpack was as close as he would ever come to Victoria Maxwell.

Drying fabric squished with a damp sound as he lifted the flap. Reaching inside, McClusky's hand experienced cool, like descending into a coal mine. Stupid, he thought. That's all my imagination. This thing's been on dry land long enough to warm up.

He removed a small ball of clothes wrapped in a plastic bag: underwear, socks and a white t-shirt. A toothbrush and miniature toothpaste tube were sealed in a ziplock baggie. A couple pens, a pulpy yellow mishmash that might once have been a legal pad. A blue plastic sleeve, wallet size, creased with transparent pockets on either side. Unfolding it, one flap was empty. The other held an ID card for the University at Buffalo, and behind it, a tattered five-dollar bill, soft and loosened.

From re-reading files, McClusky knew that Victoria's driver's license was discovered in the glove compartment of her Oldsmobile, parked at Hamburg Beach. Next to it were a pair of men's gloves, likely belonging to Tony Davenport. Why would he not take them? Had he worn a different pair onto the lake? And why did Victoria leave her license yet carry student ID?

He slid the UB card from its sleeve and flicked its edge with a thumb. Thick plastic, the texture of a credit card, with a magnetic strip across its back. Victoria's name, birth date and student number split space with a square, one inch picture.

September 10, 1967. Victoria was two years older than his daughter. Maybe that was one of the reasons this case bothered him — the three victims were just about Megan's age. He may have felt paternal toward them. When Megan reached her twenties, she was young enough that he still wanted to protect her, old enough to know that even the best parent couldn't shield a daughter from every peril in the world. Not at that age. Not anymore.

Back in 1994, he felt an affinity for these kids. But for a few years, they could have been his own.

Amazing condition this stuff is in, considering it's been underwater so long, he thought. The river is a vacuum seal.

McClusky studied Victoria's head shot. Her hair was dark blonde, parted down the middle, with long strands tucked behind her ears. Eyes were bright, set atop a thin nose and smooth cheeks. Hers was an easy, absent-minded smile. Shoulders crept toward her head awkwardly, as if she shrugged just before the photo was snapped.

Pretty girl, he mused. No fussing with makeup.

A seam ran inside the canvas flap, where a pocket was camouflaged. McClusky peeled back the overlapping fabric and peered inside. There was a stick of deodorant and another zipped baggie, containing Q-tips and a creased envelope. He removed them both, setting the deodorant on his desk. He unsealed the plastic. The envelope had no markings on its outside. McClusky slid a single sheet of paper from within, unfolding it to discover a letter. Cursive words, blue ink, curlicue handwriting suggesting a female author even before he read the signed initial:

Dear Tony:

Never write a letter in anger, isn't that the old cliché? Well, I'm ignoring that sage advice and putting pen to paper anyway. I may never give this to you, so I'm not sure if you'll ever see these words, but right now I need to write them for my own sanity.

It's only been a few weeks, but already you've filled an abscess in my heart — a void I didn't know existed until you came along. Crooking my leg over your knee as you lie on your back... putting my palm against your shoulder while you sleep... brushing thick curly hair back from your temples... these are all things I've come to treasure during the short time we've been together.

But it's been more than that. It's that slow, easy contentment you come to appreciate as an adult. It's finding comfort in another. It's not worrying about being the person someone else hopes you are. It's not about trying to aspire to be someone better. It's just being relaxed. Being me. You have given that to me.

But then comes a late-night confession that you shared something special with Amy. Suddenly complex emotions tumbled through obstacles. I feel like that little marble in Kerplunk. You pull the plastic stick, and I hit the bottom with an awful thwack.

I'm hurt, angry and betrayed. I don't know if I can trust you anymore. I'm probably over-reacting, but I'm not going to stifle my feelings, ugly as they may be.

Why did I not know about this? Why did both you and Amy keep this information from me for almost a year? Did she not tell me because she's pining for you, hoping that you'll be hers once her mourning ends?

Now I'm questioning my judgment, wondering about the wisdom of my choices. If you've been carrying this around, how well do I really know you? What other secrets are lurk-

ing behind your dark eyes?

Most importantly, where do we go from here? How do I manage to accept this about you? Can I ever be fully content with you, especially knowing that you and my best friend have shared those special moments which I thought were reserved only for me?

Can you understand why I'm upset? The phone keeps ringing tonight, and you keep leaving messages, but I don't want to talk. I can't. Maybe tomorrow will bring a fresh perspective, but right now I don't know how to get past this.

V.

McClusky's neck felt like drying plaster. From their investigation, he knew Victoria Maxwell was dating Tony Davenport, but this was curious. The letter was not dated, referring only to "last night." Had they been feuding? Had Davenport ever read these words? It seemed unlikely, considering it was sealed in a watertight bag in her backpack. If Victoria had given it to him, wouldn't he have read it and tucked it into his pocket? McClusky wondered: did they slip into a watery grave angry at each other?

"How did these kids die?" he wondered aloud, rubbing a palm along his temples. "What the hell went wrong out there? Who was the last person alive?"

30

30

When Amy Black was sixteen, a high school classmate named Kara Matsen committed suicide. The girls had not sat at the same lunch table, talked on the phone or traded gossip about boys. In fact, they had never spoken. Amy only knew Kara by sight — she was the short, petite girl who was reluctant to participate in fifth period gym. Amy sensed the girl somehow felt she was above physical education. Kara ran with a different clique — rich kids who drove their parents' expensive cars to school, smoked cigarettes in the bathroom between bells, and drank too much at weekend parties. Those kids felt entitled to material goods, and tried to act ten or even twenty years older than their age.

Facts were sketchy, leaked out in juicy increments at school on that Monday in March, beginning in homeroom: at a party Saturday night, Kara got into an argument with her best friend, then quarreled loudly with her boyfriend. Storming out, she was last seen walking down a residential street alone. With a clear view of the town's Catholic church, Kara snuck into a darkened grove of trees sometime after 1 a.m. Knotting shoelaces together, she looped a noose over a mature oak branch and hung herself. Her body was discovered dangling the following morning.

There was requisite sympathy for Kara's boyfriend, who was not seen in school the remainder of the year. The friend with whom she argued attended class as usual, remaining tight-lipped about the incident. Amy would see her talking to other girls at her locker, laughing and jovial, with no outward signs that tragedy occurred. But many suspected the girl masked her true feelings when in public. At home, in the quiet confines of her room, Amy imagined a hunched figure weeping for her lost friend, regretting harsh words which proved to be their last.

Effects of suicide rippled through the middle-class suburb. Immediately, a memorial fund was created, establishing a scholarship. Several parents challenged the board of education on how such an incident could occur, but the brain trust unearthed no clear answers. In Amy's confirmation class, round-table discussions focused on facts, rumors and innuendoes. In weeks following, suicide and its aftermath became regular topics.

The minister's premise was this: life is a sacred gift from God. It is a thing that only He should create or dispose. He has entrusted life to us; therefore, because of our love to Him, we should not betray that trust by abandoning His gift.

One of Amy's fellow confirmation candidates asked if a person who commits suicide is doomed to hell. The minister inhaled and paused, searching for precise words.

"I know that some religions teach that," he offered slowly. "We believe that to intentionally take human life is a sin. Suicide is taking your own life, therefore, logically, it is a sin."

"But it's your choice," the boy argued. "It's your body."

The minister raised a hand to stifle the interruption. "Your body is God's creation. Yes, it's yours to use in this life, but we believe it's on loan from God." He paused again, gathering words to continue his explanation. His timbre suddenly changed, as if he had thrown away text from a prepared speech. "I guess what I'm saying is this… For any person to take his own life, he must feel like all other options are dreadful. He must feel like killing himself is the absolute last resort. He must struggle with anguish and suffering in a way that most of us, thank God, will never experience.

"But rather than focus on the theological question of the degree of sin in suicide, I always feel compassion, even pity, that the person who took his own life felt so despondent and alone. I think the real hell is the state the victim is living in before he kills himself. Somewhere along the way, we, as Christians, have failed that person. We failed to make a connection so that victim — and I intentionally use that word victim — had no one to turn to so the suffering was alleviated. In my mind, that's the real sin… that someone can feel so alone that suicide is the best option."

* * *

Saturday, February 19, 1994 | 4:32 p.m.

And now, a dozen years later, Amy Black was overwhelmed by those feelings. Tony and Victoria had disappeared into Lake Erie, and had been gone long enough that she knew they would not surface. Aloneness pounded her brain, raced along her spine, burrowed inside veins. Standing on ice, she felt like a gutted trout, bones turned to warm butter. There was no one left for her — not her father, not her best friend, not her roommate. Her mother was committing some twisted perversion with a disturbed neighbor. The world held nothing honest or true anymore.

"The hurt is too much," Amy said out loud, ignoring that neither Tony nor Victoria could hear. "I can't take it. I forgive you. Of course I forgive you. It would have taken time, but I would have accepted this. I would have been happy you're in love."

Vision turned foggy; her eyes lacked focus. Land was ahead of her, she knew, and could see Canada's outline, but details that had been sharp earlier — wood-slatted shutters, blackened windows, evergreen branches — turned blurry and washed out. Her head spun with drunkenness.

She recalled Christ's final words on the cross, understanding His despondency. She spoke them aloud, imploring heaven: "My God, my God, why have you forsaken me?"

Christ's only relief was death, she thought. After His scourging, there was nothing left for Him on earth. Surrendering His body, He ascended to heaven to reunite with His father.

This has been my path to Gethsemane. Lake Erie is my Skull Place. Like Jesus, I have nothing to live for anymore. There is nothing this world could offer me which would ever soothe the pain. I could surrender my body, descend into the frigid water, and be reunited with my dad and Tony and Victoria.

Suicide is a sin, her moral voice argued.

Yet who would know? God and me, that's all. My mother, my sister, my students… no one will ever fathom that I ended my own life.

Why not wait to be rescued?

I don't want to be rescued. I don't deserve it. I'll never be able to exist knowing my friends died while I stood by, helpless to save them. How could I wake up every morning or go to sleep each night with that on my conscience?

Amy heard the minister's words from a dozen years earlier: "A suicide victim must struggle with anguish and suffering in a way that most of us will never experience."

You're damn right, she thought. You have no idea.

A few more minutes of suffering.

A few minutes of cold.

Then…

An immaculate payoff.

Admittance to heaven.

A blessed reunion.

* * *

Although she was unaware of it, a transformation occurred in Amy Black's posture. She stood straighter. Hunched shoulders rolled back, her stature commanding dignity and conviction. Arms hung loosely at her sides; neck and jaw relaxed. She felt calm, relieved. An escape route had materialized before her. Her soul became elevated, bursting from a cocoon. She suddenly became beautiful, like an actress flooded within a spotlight. Amy Black regained control of a life that had spun away from her eleven months earlier.

* * *

The decision was easier to make than follow through.

Once I go in, it's irreversible.

Amy Black inched toward the serrated opening. Water gurgled beneath its edges, tiny waves hypnotic without rhythm. A tranquil sky, empty of all color except shades of blue, contrasted with turmoil in Amy's mind.

Scared to make the leap.

Maybe I won't have to. Maybe if I step close to the edge, ice will shatter around me like it did with Tony and Victoria. I'll collapse without having to make the conscious choice… Convince myself I'm searching for my friends. Fate will be in God's hands.

Tentative steps nudged her closer to open water. Teeth clenched; she braced for the cracking sound, preparing to be swallowed by cold. But even as toes of her boots peeked over water, ice held firm.

I'm not falling, she lamented. I can't even die. Why should this be easy?

She released a plaintive sigh.

It's the right thing to do, but I'm not getting any help.

So do it.

Do it.

Do it!

She inhaled deeply, spring air misting her lips, filling nostrils with crisp evergreen scents. Steeling nerves, she thought, I'm coming home.

Eyes remained open, locked on the landscape and rooflines of nearby shore.

"God forgive me," Amy whispered.

She stepped forward.

* * *

Saturday, February 19, 1994 | 5:17 p.m.

Water gurgled in burps, churning beneath cracked ice. Close to Canada's shore, a crow leaped from its perch atop a high evergreen branch, flapping wings the sound of a razor being stropped against leather. It squawked twice before lazily circling the frozen field. Gliding, its ochre eyes scanned the vista below.

A crumbled mound caught its attention, so the bird swooped low, extending talons to land, folding dark wings under itself as it stood. Beak bobbing, waddling forward tentatively, the crow cocked its head. Fading daylight reflected a silvery shine from the pocket of a green vest. A granola bar peeked from within a torn plastic wrapper. The crow emitted another squawk, pecking its beak. Oats, splintered from the whole, were hastily devoured.

Seeing this, two more crows landed twenty feet away and marched timidly ahead, hoping for scraps, but the discoverer was not anxious to share. It cawed loudly in warning, then expanded wings to intimidate. The two scavengers leaped backwards, pausing, then resumed inching toward the bounty.

Alternately pecking and scooping up the flying oats with greed, the first crow bent its head low, grasping food within its black beak. But the granola bar was wedged into the pocket. The bird had neither the ability nor dexterity to remove it. To ensure the invaders were not rewarded, it pinched the vest within its beak and skittered away, dragging the coat across ice.

This did not deter the other crows. They followed at a cautious distance, so the bird clamped a firm grip, flapped wings and took to air, flying mere feet above the horizon with a green vest dangling limply from its beak. Awkwardly, slowed by the encumbrance, it dropped the vest several hundred feet from its original position.

Landing quickly, the crow continued to protect its treasure, pecking and dragging the loot until granola was finely chopped and oats had all been swallowed.

31

31

Mark Jablonski's blog
Posted Thursday, February 19, 2004

Sitting on the southern shore of a Canadian beach, the view of Buffalo across Lake Erie is unfamiliar to my American eyes. I've never witnessed this angle, behind a frozen tundra of ice and snow. From this vantage, much of the city is hidden, the landscape dominated instead by the Skyway's arching bridge and mills of the old Bethlehem Steel plant.

I don't know why I came here, or what I expect to see. The beach is deserted. The only signs of life are fading paw prints pressed into snow. I'm fairly certain I won't perceive three ghostly spirits, walking across the lake in an opaque glare of white on white.

Right about now, ten years ago, my best friend, his girlfriend, and her roommate began a daylong adventure by walking across this expanse before me.

On that fateful Saturday in 1994, it was unseasonably

warm. This did not deter their quest. Ice was frozen thickly enough, they believed, that a day or two of warmth could not possibly melt layers away or jeopardize their safety. It was a fatal mistake. They departed from Hamburg Beach around noon, aiming for the Canadian shore. No one ever heard from them again.

The consensus in the aftermath of their disappearance was that they should have known better. These were educated people, after all. Tony Davenport, my pal, was three months away from earning a master's degree in English. He taught as a substitute in local high schools and wanted to be a full-time teacher. Victoria Maxwell, his new girlfriend, was enrolled in UB's law school. Amy Black, Victoria's roommate who was also a close friend of Tony's, was living Tony's dream job — she taught high school, although her subject area was art.

Tony was only twenty-five years old; Victoria, twenty-six. Amy, suffering depression from her dad's passing the previous March, was twenty-eight.

These were three people who, by fate or the inexplicable will of a higher power, were taken from this world before they had time to realize their true potential.

There isn't a day that has passed in the last decade when I haven't considered Tony, and by extension, Amy and Victoria. Today, on the shores of a wintry beach, I wonder again: had they lived, where would they be now? How would the planet be a better place by having them on it? What would they be doing?

In my writer's fantasy, I can create an alternate reality...

Tony should be thirty-five, and although it's pure speculation, I believe he and Victoria would have married. In one of our final conversations, he confided how smitten he was with her. This was unlike Tony. Until then, girls were simply a happy diversion. But he and Victoria had been friends before romance blossomed, so he was confident the feelings were legitimate.

Tony would be teaching. He'd be the head of an English department at a suburban high school. Kids would be drawn to his genuineness and accessibility. Having influenced several hundred students in his years of teaching, he would have at least one "Teacher of the Year" plaque hanging on his classroom wall.

Victoria would be on partner track at a small, independent law firm in the city. Large out of town companies would have wooed her, but she liked living in Western New York. Originally from Ohio, she discovered a comfort here, and the love of a good man. She would employ her sense of justice in Buffalo, her adopted hometown. Now thirty-six, she would be an advocate for family issues, securing the rights of children in a world that too often neglects the underprivileged.

On warm summer nights, Tony and Victoria would come to my house. In the backyard, I'd fire up the grill and cook burgers and dogs. My wife would toss fresh vegetables into the salads she loves to make. Tony and I would sit on the patio, sipping beer like we did all those years ago, and talk about our daily hopes and dreams. As the sun set, Tony and Victoria's two kids would play with ours.

Amy's would-be life is more difficult to concoct. Squinting through the haze, I believe the depression that gripped her final months would have evaporated, and she would have returned to the person we knew before. To everyone's growing concern, she had begun spending too much time by herself. She often stayed alone at the family's cottage in Fort Erie, just down the road from where I stand. Her dad's death triggered a withdrawal. Tony, more than anyone, made a consistent effort to keep her connected with the world. At the time of her death, I don't know whether she had yet to bottom out, or if the recovery process had begun.

Because of the disappearance of my friends, I understand and sympathize with her struggles around loss in a way I never did when they were alive.

Amy was a good person who was swallowed, temporarily, by bad circumstances. She would have continued teaching, and fallen in love with an opposite personality — a business or science teacher at her school, perhaps. Now 38, only recently married, she and her man would have traveled the globe, visiting exotic locales like Angkor Wat and Papua New Guinea. On the home front, they would be lobbying Albany to preserve rural open spaces or ensure teacher benefits. Knowing Amy, she would continue the path she began before her father's death sidetracked her: actively trying to shape a better society.

Three deaths... what a loss to consider what could have been.

Recently, I broke my self-imposed silence (for although I feel empowered by writing I am reluctant to give voice to my feelings about Tony) and told the story of my friends' deaths to a young co-worker. He seemed puzzled. "Why didn't they just call 911 for help if they got stuck?" he asked. "Didn't they take a cell phone?"

Although they were around in 1994, cell phones were new technology, their use not nearly as prolific as today. No, they did not have a cell phone, flares, life preservers or ropes. They did not pack the proper equipment for such an adventure. For a long time, as I struggled with the healing process, that angered me.

I felt frustrated and helpless about Tony's death for a long time, and that morphed to guilt. He called me Friday, the night before departing, and told me of the planned hike. "Are you sure it's safe?" I asked. "The weatherman says it's going to be warm tomorrow."

"Do you know how thick that ice is?" he answered. "If we see any weak spots, we'll go around them, or turn back."

I later learned the impossibility of detecting weak spots in ice simply by looking. At the time, I didn't press the issue of safety. If I had, perhaps my friends would still be alive. Guilt is a heavy overcoat.

But time allows life to create order. I'm a different person than I was in 1994. Then, at 25, I was fickle, yearning for self-importance. Tony's death awakened me to life's fragility. I stopped trying to impress others, and started to live responsibly. I met a girl named Melinda, fell in love, and married her in 1998. Physically, Tony was absent from the wedding, where he would have been best man. In spirit, his personality glowed throughout the day.

As my young colleague pointed out, so much of the world has changed. I'm not sure it's for the better. Now we have cell phones, internet, DVDs, terrorism. We have hockey in Florida, a war in Iraq, SUVs with TVs in the backseat. How would Tony and Victoria and Amy have adapted?

Ten years later, I scour my soul for answers.

Speculation…

Lives that should have been longer, more completed…

Tony, my friend, in my right hand I hold a ten-year-old bottle of scotch. My left contains a small tumbler. I crack the bottle's seal and pour three fingers in your memory, toasting a long-gone confidant. The landscape before me is desolate and deserted, but a decade ago you were leading man in the scene. Somewhere on the horizon before me, the exact location known only to God, you lived your last moments.

The amber scotch tastes thick and silky as it coats the back of my throat.

The drink does not make me feel better.

I want to say so many things, but words are inadequate. I want to reach across lost years and bask in your jovial, easy-going presence again. Those were happy days we spent together, in a time more innocent and naive. Know this: when you exhaled that final breath, my world became a lonelier place.

I love you, I miss you, and I won't ever forget.

Acknowledgements

There are many people affiliated with Frontier High School who contributed to this book. Its genesis was a lunchtime conversation with Mark Pogodzinski and Krista Sacco. Veteran teachers Dave Ceccerelli, Ron Schranz and Mark Chavel all used their contacts to open doors during research. Librarian Esther Kowal is a jewel. I asked for information and she delivered without fail, continuously over several years. Steve Miller made editing suggestions. Nancy Witteman read an early draft and the final draft and provided insightful comments, while Linda Rayburg shared her own story of being stuck on Lake Erie's ice. Her memories found their way into this fiction. Nicole Haberer adapted the design of an alternate book cover. Students helped as well: Kaylei Mittner recounted her experiences on jade-colored ice far from shore, while Tom Morgan and Shannon Pershyn offered feedback and encouragement. Josh Jezioro wrote an adapted screenplay and began filming while I was still writing. This forced me to push ahead, and our discussions helped define the characters. Former student Alex Turnwall designed the cover and coordinated the book's layout.
Captain Kevin Caffery of the Erie County Sheriff's

Department provided an inside look at helicopter rescues, and I called on Tony Kozlowski and Richard Smith for their vast knowledge of Lake Erie. Steve Desmond set me straight about the difference between "pictures" and "photos," while the Buffalo Office of the National Weather Service determined precise data for specific dates.

At the 2006 New York State Summer Writers Institute, in a workshop directed by Rick Moody, discussion about the early chapters provided me with an array of critical questions. The book was strengthened thanks to Moody and my classmates.

Tom Roberts read an early draft and offered praise, which encouraged me to continue. Tobi Stewart did the same thing, and I am indebted to her for suggesting the book's title. Other helpful feedback came from Wynne Everett, Donna Laudico and the Bauer family: Ronni, Rob, Bill and Michele, who listened to me plot out details while we built their house in the summer of 2005.

As always, I am humbled by the love of my parents, Tom and Mary Jo, my aunt, Marcia McCarthy, and my better half, Melanie Smith.

About the Author

Jeff Schober attended Bowling Green State University and the University at Buffalo. He has written for several Western New York publications on a wide range of topics, from sports to politics to book reviews, and has acted in several Shakespeare plays in Southern Ontario. He is an English teacher at Frontier High School in Hamburg, New York. This is his first novel.

ISBN 142513812-8

9 781425 138127